The Quickening

e Myerson is the author of thirteen books.

n her fiction, she finds herself drawn to the super-
 ural again and again, and especially to ghosts. She
 only ever once seen one herself. On a freezing
 ter's night in 1984, a small, ragged, white-faced boy
 ked into the bedroom of the house where she was
 ying. She screamed and he disappeared. But he crept
 her first novel, *Sleepwalking*, and was, she hopes, laid
 est on its pages.

She began watching Friday night Hammer Horror
 ovies as a teenager in the 1970s, loves the ghost
 ries of Edith Wharton and MR James, but thinks
 enry James' *The Turn of the Screw* is probably the most
 ightening thing she has ever read.

She lives in London.

'I found it to be genuinely scary and enthralling. Myerson's gift for breathing life into her characters is so effective that I worried passionately about Rachel and Dan'
Spectator

'It's a good fast read; just the thing for your next Caribbean holiday.'
Evening Standard

'Tense and terrifying'
Woman and Home

By the same author

Julie
Myerson

The
Quickening

HAMMER
AN EXCLUSIVE MEDIA COMPANY

Published by Arrow Books in association with Hammer 2014

1 3 5 7 9 10 8 6 4 2

First published in Great Britain in 2013 by
Arrow Books in association with Hammer
The Random House Group Limited
20 Vauxhall Bridge Road, London, SW1V 2SA

www.randomhouse.co.uk

Addresses for companies within The Random House Group Limited can be found at:
www.randomhouse.co.uk/offices.htm

The Random House Group Limited Reg. No. 954009

A CIP catalogue record for this book
is available from the British Library

ISBN 9780099580249

The Random House Group Limited supports the Forest Stewardship Council®
(FSC®), the leading international forest-certification organisation. Our books carrying
the FSC label are printed on FSC®-certified paper. FSC is the only forest-certification
scheme supported by the leading environmental organisations, including Greenpeace.
Our paper procurement policy can be found at:
www.randomhouse.co.uk/environment

Typeset in Centaur MT by SX Composing DTP, Rayleigh, Essex, SS6 7XF
Printed and bound by CPI Group (UK) Ltd, Croydon, CR0 4YY

For Mum, Nick and Buddy
with a lot of love

The
Quickening

Chapter One

Rachel and Dan wanted to go somewhere hot in January or February. It was already early January, so they were looking for last-minute deals online. Rachel said she fancied Florida, but Dan said he'd fallen right out of love with the States.

The Canary Islands, then?

Dan pushed a hand inside the still-loose top of her jeans, the place where they'd recently discovered their baby was growing.

Have you any idea how tacky places like Tenerife and Lanzarote are?

Rachel smiled. When she was ten, her best friend had gone on holiday to Tenerife. To Rachel – who, because of her father's condition, had never been abroad and spent most of her holidays in a grim, unheated mansion in the Scottish Highlands – it had sounded like a trip to the moon.

The friend had brought her back a souvenir, a fat plastic biro which, when you tipped it back and forth, caused an impossibly small ship to slide around in an eerie bubble of liquid. Tenerife. She still thought about that biro sometimes.

How about Jamaica? Dan said.

Rachel made a face.

Isn't it supposed to be rough and violent?

All right, then, Barbados?

She felt herself tense. When they first got together, Dan went to Sandy Lane on a press trip. He told her that no one was taking wives or girlfriends, but later she discovered it wasn't true. They had a row about it. Their first proper fight. But it wasn't the fight she minded, it was the lie. She didn't want to think about that now. But she thought he might have had the tact not to suggest Barbados.

She twisted on the sofa, nudging his hand off her belly.

Barbados seems a bit obvious, she said. All those rich people.

Dan raised an eyebrow, but she shrugged. She didn't think or feel or behave like someone with money and she knew she never would.

All right, then. How about this? Dan had his lap-top propped on his knees and was stroking her thigh with one hand and scrolling down with the other. 'Tucked away on a secluded 100-acre peninsula on the south-eastern coast of Antigua, the Wyndham's Club and Resort exudes a casual, luxurious ambience – '

Rachel leaned over to look.

Antigua? That's the Caribbean?

He grinned.

Last time I looked, I think that's where it was. Luxurious seclusion. Mmm. I like the sound of that, don't you?

Something about the way he said it made Rachel look at him.

You've been there?

He blinked.

Never in my whole life, m'lud, I swear. Though I bet it's not a lot different from Barbados. But listen, how do you fancy: six swimming pools, four restaurants, two white-sand beaches, tennis courts, a spa – '

Rachel sat up.

Let me see, she said. The beaches. Let me see them.

Dan clicked. She saw blue, green, white. Palm trees. A bay drowning in sunshine. Light so bright you could taste it. She stared at the screen –

What? Dan said. What is it?

She could not breathe. Her heart was thumping. She put her hand to her throat, gulped in air.

Dan was staring at her.

What on earth was that?

She swallowed. Her blood was still jumping. She felt like she wanted to cry.

I don't know, she said.

He laid a hand on her shoulder. She wanted to shrug it off, but she didn't.

All right now?

She nodded, dared herself to look back at the screen. Dan refreshed it. The colours glowed. Antigua.

Could we really afford that? she said.

Maybe partly because of her mother's attitude to him, Dan refused to have anything to do with the money her father had left her. And she respected that. But now, with newspapers cutting costs all over the place, he wasn't earning a lot.

He had his column of course, and these days was increasingly known as a film critic. But who knew when all of that might dry up? He talked about writing a book. But Dan talked about a lot of things and even she knew that advances were tiny these days. And though she loved her work and even had plans one day to open a gallery of her own, it was hardly well paid and she couldn't say what would happen when the baby came along.

Dan grinned. Something in his eyes was still bothering her.

OK, he said. I'm going to have to come clean. We can and we already have.

Have? What do you mean, have?

Afforded it.

Rachel stared at him.

I booked it yesterday, he said.

You – what? That place? You mean you went and booked it? Without even asking me?

Dan's eyes widened.

Yes, Rach. Without asking you. I think it's what most people would call a romantic gesture.

OK, she said.

He reached over and tucked a piece of hair behind her ear.

What is it? What's the matter?

Nothing, she said.

I hope it's nothing. Because, since I was in a shopping mood, I also splashed out on something else. Shut your eyes.

She did as he said. Felt the sofa cushions shift as he wriggled to get something from his pocket. When at last he told her she could look, she saw that he was holding his two fists out in front of her. Her heart lurched.

Which hand?

She bit her lip. Gently, she tapped his left knuckle. He opened the hand, turned it over.

Wrong as usual.

He laughed. Then he leaned in to kiss her and, opening his other hand, he slipped it onto her finger. She felt its coldness and looked down and saw the flash of gold, the tiny diamond pointing upwards.

Oh Dan, she said.

She wiped her fingers, made moist by the touch of his, on her jeans, then straight away felt guilty. He was nervous. Dan was never nervous. She felt a rush of love.

She turned her hand, watching the jewel suck at the light.

But I thought we were going to wait, she said. Till after the baby?

His eyes were unreadable. He put a hand on her knee.

I know, he said. I know we were. But — well, you know, Rach — something about this last couple of weeks —

Just before Christmas, one of Dan's oldest friends had been killed. Everything had just started to go well for Rufus. After years of no work, he'd got the second lead in a big-budget TV detective series. The first series had been a success and they were making another. And he and Natasha had just moved to Kent. After three rounds of IVF, they were expecting twins.

They'd been putting up the tree – their first Christmas tree together – when Dan got the call. Rachel had watched as he listened for a moment and then, a piece of tinsel still hanging from his hand, climbed down the ladder.

Something about the way he moved – suddenly slow and frail as an old man, feeling for each step with his foot – made her stop what she was doing. She moved over and sat down beside him on the sofa, clutched at his arm. What? she mouthed. What?

It had happened the previous night. The car had skidded off the road and hit a metal gate. A farm gate, Tash told them. He'd been killed instantly.

He'd got four days off from filming, she told Dan, her voice still blank with shock. He was so looking forward to a break. And we were supposed to be going for a scan today. Our second scan. We'd planned it so he could be there. I'd just spoken to him. He was less than ten minutes from home.

Now Dan looked at Rachel.

I don't see the point of waiting, do you? I love you, Rach. I want to be married to you.

I love you too, she said. But —

But what?

She looked at his face.

But nothing, she said.

He brightened.

So tomorrow morning you put on your glad rags and we pop down the register office, make an honest woman of you. Then you've a day to pack your bags and buy a bikini. We fly on Saturday, crack of dawn.

Her mouth fell open.

You mean get married all on our own? Without our friends? And my mum — what about my mum?

He took her hand in his and kissed the tips of her fingers.

I don't want anyone there. Please, Rachel. I want it to be just us. Our thing. Our secret. We'll have our honeymoon. You'll even have your birthday there. And then, when we come back, we'll throw a huge party for everyone. A birthday party and a wedding party and a baby party all in one. As many people as you like. Your mum as guest of honour.

Rachel struggled to imagine it.

We'll even get you a white dress. Think how sexy you'll look, with a tan.

He kissed her.

Look, I know I've been slow. About everything. I've been wasting time. Even the baby – especially the baby – I know it's taken me a while to get used to the whole thing. But I'm looking forward to it now. I'm sorry.

There's nothing to be sorry about, she said.

But I am. I'm sorry about everything. I love you so much, Rach.

They kissed again. They were still at the stage when a kiss could last for a minute or so.

But seriously, she said when she finally extracted herself and took his arms and wrapped them tight around her. That place looks expensive. I thought we said we were going to try and find a last-minute package deal or something?

Dan reached over and took a sip of his cold tea.

Well, all right, I didn't want to say. But I did stoop to using a couple of contacts.

Oh – her face fell again – but you haven't got to write about it, have you?

The number of times she'd tried to enjoy a dinner or a weekend away, only to have him constantly stopping to make notes about it.

Of course I haven't. Bloody hell. It's my honey-moon too, isn't it? Stop panicking, Rach. Let's just say we're getting quite a good deal, that's all. They'll take care of us.

She squeezed his hand.

All right, she said.

She watched his face, thought she detected the faintest sliver of hurt.

Sorry I was mean about it, she said.

You weren't mean.

I was.

Don't be silly. You could never be mean.

All the same. I'm sorry.

He kissed her.

See? he said, as she relaxed against him. I really have thought of everything. It's all fixed, all done. I want it to be perfect. I love you so much, Rach.

Perfect. Yes. It was what she wanted too. She thought of her baby, tipping back and forth some-where inside her in its bubble of liquid. Eerie. Intact. Like the tiny ship, so long ago.

Me too, she said. I love you too.

They got married in a Georgian room with a high, ornate ceiling and a stained red carpet and were congratulated afterwards by three strangers they knew they would never see again. Then they went home and took a bottle of champagne to bed – half a glass for her because of the baby, which meant practically a whole bottle for him. After he'd pleasured her so hard that she trembled for what she swore was a whole five minutes, they ate bowlfuls of Special K with brown sugar and double cream and fell asleep in front of *Love, Actually* which was the only thing on.

Only because you just got married, Dan said as he relinquished control of the remote. But if you ever force me to watch this crap again, I'm filing for instant divorce.

On Saturday morning they left a cold and rainy Gatwick at dawn and by four o'clock that afternoon were standing under a bamboo awning by the Sugar Bay Dive Shop, listening to a steel band and holding glasses of rum punch.

They weren't the only ones who'd just arrived. There were some people who'd been on their flight and shared the hotel mini-bus from the airport – a dusty drive past run-down shacks and skinny, barely clothed kids who stood and waved to them from the side of the road.

Dan – sitting up in the front next to the driver – had asked if there was much poverty on the island.

Keeping his eyes on the road, the driver nodded.

Poverty is big problem in Antigua and Barbuda.

Many people with nothing to eat. My own children are very often hungry.

What? – Rachel saw that Dan had his journalist face on – You mean your own family doesn't have enough to eat?

The driver glanced at him.

Sometimes only rice and cornmeal pap for dinner. Sometimes nothing.

Dan sighed. He looked out of the window.

But tourism? It's a good thing? It brings in money? For local people, I mean?

The driver looked at him again, then switched his eyes back to the road. There was a brief silence and then he said something which Rachel didn't catch, but which Dan must have heard, because his face grew tense.

No, he said. Never in my life.

The driver said something else. Dan shook his head.

It's not possible, he said.

Rachel leaned forward in her seat.

What's he saying?

Dan glanced back at her.

Nothing, darling. Just us getting our wires crossed.

But Rachel grabbed his shoulder.

Tell me. Tell me what he said.

He rolled his eyes.

Oh, it really isn't important. Just something about him thinking he's seen me here before.

Rachel looked at the driver and then at Dan.

But you've never been here.

Exactly what I told him.

But the driver caught Rachel's eye in the mirror.

Your husband is here on this island, he said.

Rachel tried to laugh.

Here? Well, of course he's here.

The driver's face was serious.

Not now, he said. Always. He cannot leave.

Dan laughed.

Well, if I've got to be stuck somewhere – better here than south-east London.

But Rachel felt her heart start to race.

What do you mean? she said. Always? That makes no sense.

The driver did not look at her. His eyes were on the road.

I am only saying. It is a warning.

Rachel looked at the road too. Dust clouds all around the car. A petrified tree. A couple of oil drums.

A warning about what? she said.

But the driver said nothing. Already they were

sweeping through the dark wrought-iron gates of the resort. A minute later, their luggage was whisked away and they were standing under the awning, being handed cool, damp perfumed towels and cocktails by girls with flowers in their hair.

Rachel held her towel to her wrists, her throat. The scent of flowers was in the air. Blossom and something aromatic like eucalyptus. The rattle of cicadas. The light was silky, the afternoon sky high and blue and cloudless.

She looked around for Dan and saw that he was talking to a youngish, pretty woman in a halter-neck dress. She had huge gold hoops in her ears. Her boyfriend – if he was her boyfriend – had his greying hair pulled back in a ponytail. She knew just by looking at them that they were English.

She decided not to go over. She was tired and crumpled from the plane and didn't feel like talking to anyone. She wished they could just go straight to their room. She wanted to wash. She wanted to find the beach.

She saw that Dan and his friends had now been joined by a large woman of about seventy, whose white sweatpants and raffia sandals had seemed ridiculous when she noticed them in the lounge at grey, freezing Gatwick, but who now looked quite at home as she helped herself to another drink.

Karen Keable, Rachel heard someone call her. She could tell from the way the manager greeted them that she and her husband – an unhappy-looking wisp of a man – were regulars here.

She took a couple of sips of the punch, then, worried about the alcohol, swapped it for something that looked like pineapple juice. Or was it papaya? Its acid taste set her teeth on edge and made her stomach growl. She hadn't been able to face the food on the plane and now she thought about it, she realised she'd had nothing since the two bites of Dan's Pret A Manger sandwich which he'd forced her to eat at seven that morning.

Does your husband play tennis, dear? Karen Keable said.

Rachel looked at the dry, frayed coral of her lips and tried to think.

We're *Telegraph* readers. I recognised him straight away, of course. And I wondered if he played. Because Malcolm over there, who between you and me is no great shakes, is always on the look-out for a partner.

Rachel was about to tell her that yes, Dan did play tennis and would probably love to – a quick, guilty vision of herself left in peace under an umbrella on the beach — when, as suddenly as if someone had just reached out and flicked a switch, the air around her, the sunshine, the blue brightness, it was all gone —

She froze.

Are you all right, dear? You don't look very well at all. Is it the heat, do you think? Do you need to sit down?

Karen Keable's words were so distant that she knew she needn't bother listening. She shut her eyes and let the air get ready to catch her. Just before she fell, Dan was there.

Darling — honey, what's the matter?

Then the manager was behind her with a chair. She felt herself manoeuvred into it.

A long flight, no?

He was a man in a white suit. He bent towards her. She smelled a strong aftershave. The sad odour of his body beneath it.

Just a touch of low blood pressure, she heard Dan say. She's pregnant, you see.

Pregnant. Yes, that was it. Rachel blinked. Grateful. The warmth and the light seeping back.

And then everything else, too, returning. The rattle of the cicadas. The voices. Dan. Karen Keable.

Pregnant, someone was saying. But that's wonder -

ful. Is it your first? How very exciting —

They were celebrating her.

Water, someone else said.

Water was fetched. And another icy towel pressed to her head. Even the woman in the halter-neck dress was crouching by her chair, the great gold hoops of her earrings swinging in the late-afternoon sunshine.

How far along are you? she said. Do you know?

Fourteen weeks, Rachel said.

She'd known the very moment she conceived. An off-balance feeling. Dan had laughed at her. But the pregnancy test a couple of weeks later had told her she was right. It was then.

Or that week anyway, Dan had said.

No, Rachel had corrected him. That day.

You can't possibly know that.

I can.

Something igniting inside her. A life. How could anyone doubt it? She'd never been so certain of anything.

At last the fuss subsided. She heard them all carry on with the drinking and the laughing. Forgetting about her. That was nice. And then, even nicer, a cool breeze on her neck.

It was only as the party broke up and empty glasses were put down on trays and Dan — admitting he was dying for a cigarette — pulled her to her feet, that it came back to her. The thing she'd seen.

It was human. It had black dirt on its hands. It had come to the island looking for her.

Their room was on ground level, just across the walkway from a small plunge pool where a sheet of turquoise water churned under a canopy of pink hibiscus flowers.

It had a stone-flagged floor, king-size bed, sitting area with a rattan three-piece suite, and a wrought-iron balcony looking out over the bay. It also had a generous-sized marble bathroom.

Dan put his head in.

His and hers showers, he reported. And a sex bath.

Rachel smiled. It was their private word for circular baths. A joke about some scummy hotel they'd once found themselves in in Manchester, or was it Leeds?

Dan went out on the balcony.

Not a bad view either. But it won't get the sun in the morning. And if you want to sit out here having a nightcap, everyone's going to hear every bloody word you say.

But are they occupied? Rachel said. The rooms on either side?

He shrugged.

Let's hope not. I don't want to hear other people screaming and lashing each other to the bedposts. I just want to be alone with my wife.

Rachel stood in the middle of the room and looked at the bed. It had no posts. Just a calm rattan headboard which matched the sofa and chairs.

Oh great — Dan bent to stare into the fridge. All the spirits are missing. Just some white wine, tonic water and a couple of Mars bars. I hope they aren't going to bill us for that.

Rachel looked at him.

Stop trying to find things wrong with everything.

He looked surprised.

I'm not.

You are. You keep on listing all the drawbacks. That's usually my job.

He carried on looking surprised for a moment longer. And then he laughed.

They were due at the Mangrove Lounge at 7pm. Welcome cocktails, the piece of paper said. And dinner in the Coralita Restaurant hosted by the manager.

Rachel sighed.

Is this because of you using your contacts? Are we

going to be trapped into talking to that manager guy all the time?

Dan looked up from his laptop.

It's what they always do at these places. People love it. People like your Karen Keable. It's what they come for – to be on first-name terms with the manager. But don't worry, we'll be late. And after that we'll be as stand-offish as we like for the whole holiday.

Rachel was silent.

What are you doing? she said. On the computer. What are you looking at?

He pressed a button and shut it.

Nothing. Just seeing if Natasha's been in touch.

And has she?

No.

He came over, placed his hands on her shoulders, kissed her nose.

That's nice, she said. That you're checking.

I can't help thinking about her, he said.

He went into the bathroom.

She stood there for a moment listening to the water crashing out of the taps. Then she went around the room, adjusting things and trying to make it theirs.

She took the stiff, satin monogrammed cushions

and shiny bedspread off the bed and shoved them in the top of the wardrobe. Checked to see if the mattress was firm (it was). Looked to see if there were any extra pillows (there weren't). Arranged her books and pregnancy bible and the little bottle of lavender oil on the bedside table. Her bible. He'd laughed at her for wanting to bring it on holiday, but how could she let weeks 15, 16 and 17 go by without looking to see what was happening inside her?

She found a woman's hairgrip – a single, long black hair still attached to it – on the floor under the dressing table and dropped it in the bin. She picked up the empty and now depressing suitcases and shoved them into the space at the bottom of the wardrobe. After that, drained of all energy, she kicked off her shoes and sat down on the edge of the bed.

You might want to keep the bedspread handy, you know, Dan said as he strode back in, naked and damp, and started to open the complimentary bottle of fizzy wine on the sideboard. I bet it gets fucking freezing here at night.

She sat on the bed and looked at him. Her husband. Droplets of water on his upper arms and between his shoulder blades where the towel hadn't reached. Just like at home.

She blinked.

Don't worry, she said. I brought my pyjamas.

You're not wearing pyjamas on your honeymoon, I'm telling you that right now, he said. I'll keep you warm. I'll keep both of you warm.

Both of them. Rachel loved it when he acknowledged their child as something rooted in his own life as well as in hers. They'd agreed it was too early to talk about names, but still they kept on floating into her head.

She liked Daphne. Greek, wasn't it? She'd never come across a Daphne. But then she liked Violet, too. Ruby, at a pinch. For boys she quite liked plain old-fashioned John. John! No one these days seemed to call their baby John.

What do you think of John? she said.

Dan was undoing the wire on the bottle.

What?

As a name. John. Do you like it?

He scowled.

Bloody awful. And I thought we agreed not to do this yet?

She shrugged, looked down at her bare feet on the terracotta tiles. Moist, pale little marks where her toes had been.

I don't think we're having a boy anyway, she said.

Good, said Dan.

She looked at him.

You'd like a girl?

He popped the cork.

I'll have whatever's going. But if it's a girl, she'd better be as knock-out gorgeous as you.

Rachel smiled.

I'm not gorgeous.

All right, you're not.

Well, maybe I am, she said. A bit.

She felt like talking more about the baby, but didn't want to push her luck. He poured the wine and tried to pass her a glass but she waved it away. She began to undress for her bath.

Remind me to ask for some extra pillows, she said. Or do you think I should ring for them now?

Dan was holding his glass and looking at her.

Not now, he said.

He kept his eyes on her. She knew that look.

She lifted her head and glanced out across the terrace. The light had just that moment left the sky. On the beach a single lonely figure was going along collapsing the chairs and umbrellas, one by one.

She shivered. She picked up her drink, poured half of it into Dan's glass. Then she went into the bathroom to have her bath.

*

They made love as quietly as they could in case there really were people in the room next door. She didn't think she was in the mood, but in the end she was so loud he had to put his hand over her mouth. Afterwards, she wanted to laugh, but she didn't.

When they'd finished, it was properly dark. The stars were so bright it looked like someone had torn holes in the sky.

She pulled on a stretchy mauve dress that she now realised had seen better days. She stopped to look at herself sideways in the mirror. Was she beginning to show just a little bit? She took her half-glass of fizz – still barely touched – and went and stood out on the terrace.

Above her, the night sky flashed and glittered. She put the tumbler down on the table and tipped her head back to look – so many stars, so much brightness.

Instantly the air was alive with the sound of breaking glass. Shards prickling her legs. The terrace strewn with pieces. Stricken, appalled, she gazed at the wall, wine from her glass running down the white - washed stone.

She was numb. She could not move or speak. She could not even cry out. Dan came rushing.

What the hell – ?

She was shaking all over. Trying to breathe. All she could do was point.

My glass –

He was staring at her. Barefoot in just his boxers. A toothbrush in his hand.

Darling! What's going on?

He swallowed a mouthful of toothpaste. Looked at the smashed glass all over the floor, then back at her.

What on earth did you do that for? he said.

She stared at him, still unable to move or speak.

They went back inside. She was still shaking. Her body, her teeth, everything. She held out her hand, her fingers.

How do I make it stop? she said.

She didn't know whether she meant the shaking or the thing. Dan was getting dressed. Whistling under his breath. She sat down on the bed, her knees like water.

It wasn't me, she said. You have to believe me. The glass – it was on the table. I didn't touch it.

Forget it, he said. It doesn't matter. They'll clear it up.

But I didn't touch it.

He wasn't listening. He was tipping something out of his shoe.

That is just so completely weird. I thought I felt something in there – look.

Still trembling, Rachel looked. On the floor, something round and bright and shiny and red.

He was laughing.

Would you believe it? This cherry tomato shot out of my salad on the plane – I thought it went on the floor. But it must have gone in my shoe. It's been there all this time.

Rachel stared at it. She got to her feet and bent and picked it up. She walked out onto the terrace and chucked it over the balcony rail, watched it land in the black earth just below their window.

Careful, Dan called. Remember the glass.

I've got shoes on, she said.

Out there, her voice was strange. It wasn't her voice. She shut her mouth.

She made herself look at the wall. It was already dry. But there were tiny fragments of glass everywhere. All over the tiles, under the balcony rail. The force of it. It could not have been thrown harder.

She came back in, drew the mosquito screen across for a second time, put on lipstick and a spritz of perfume, waited while Dan rolled a cigarette. Out of sheer habit, she began to straighten the bed.

What the fuck are you doing? he said, laughing at her. Don't be silly. They'll do that.

Then they put the *Please make up the room* sign on the door, locked it and, hand in hand, made their way along the moonlit walkway and down to the Coralita Restaurant for their obligatory sunset cocktail.

The manager's name was Cedric. She knew she'd end up having to sit next to him and she did. He had relatives in Muswell Hill. Did she and Dan know Muswell Hill? What were the transport links like to Muswell Hill? How long would it take to get from Muswell Hill to Morden where he had some other relatives on his mother's side?

We live in Lewisham, Rachel said, gazing past his big, shaven head at the black, moonlit ocean. It's pretty much the other side of London.

Cedric looked elated. When his mouth opened, she saw that he had a gold tooth.

Ah, but then you must go there! A special trip to Muswell Hill! When you return home, yes? You must promise me this.

Rachel looked around. Dan was miles away, right down at the other end of the table, talking to halterneck woman and ponytail man. She watched them for a moment.

Do you happen to know whether it is actually on a hill? Cedric was saying.

What? she said.

She eyed her glass, placed a finger on the base, shivered.

Muswell Hill. Is it on a hill?

Four waitresses in brown uniforms and white aprons were going around serving the food, topping up water glasses, pouring wine. Three of them were smiling – maybe they knew that Cedric was watching them – but one, the youngest one, a skinny teenager with big teeth, wasn't.

She looked agitated, even upset. At one point Rachel caught her eye and it was so intense she had to look away. Next time the girl was close, she checked the name on the badge pinned to her apron. *Hortensia*.

Hortensia held a dish while Karen Keable helped herself to some kind of spiny yellow vegetable. She waved the spoon at Rachel from across the table.

Did you have a nice rest? I do hope you're feeling much better?

Rachel told her she was.

I'm sure it was the heat. It's supposed to be even hotter tomorrow. Eighty-five degrees.

Rachel shifted in her seat. The hard cane chair was sticking to her thighs. She felt Hortensia's eyes on her.

You're probably wondering where Malcolm is, Karen Keable continued. I'm afraid he's lying low. Diarrhoea. Such a bore.

She poured sauce over her vegetables. Rachel looked away.

I'm sorry to hear that, she said.

Hortensia moved off and the next girl came along. Karen Keable helped herself to potatoes.

I was hoping I might be sat next to your hubby, she continued. We were having such an interesting chat earlier. I had no idea he was on the box as well. I'll have to look out for him now.

Oh, Rachel said. He isn't on that much. It's just an occasional thing.

Karen Keable waved away the girl who tried to offer her water. She held up her wine glass. As soon as it was filled, she beamed at Rachel.

How long are you here for, anyway?

Almost three weeks, Rachel said.

It seemed an absurdly long time to her, but Karen Keable nodded approval.

And how long have you been married?

Just a couple of days, Rachel admitted, cursing herself the moment she said it.

Karen Keable stopped, her spoon in mid-air.

You're not serious? You mean you're on honey-moon? This is your honeymoon? You hear that, Cedric? These lovely young people just got married! They're on their honeymoon right now, for goodness' sake!

Cedric's face didn't change.

What a pity. If you'd said when you booked, you could have had one of our deluxe honeymoon packages at a special discount.

Karen Keable leaned towards her.

They do all sorts of things for honeymooners here. Spa packages. Sunset cruises. Isn't that right, Cedric?

Cedric frowned.

Romance, Indulgence or Action, he said.

Indulgence – is that the one with the Couples Spa Treatments? Karen Keable said. Not that I've ever seen the point of that. Why on earth would you want to have your bits done in front of your husband?

Cedric's face didn't change.

A full body massage, he explained. Lying side by side in the same room.

Horrific, said Karen Keable.

But many people these days choose the Action and Adventure package – sailing, diving, an eco tour of the island. That's our most popular one.

Karen Keable looked at Rachel.

Can you think of anything worse than having to go round looking at rainforests on your honeymoon?

Rachel looked at her plate. Hortensia had just laid a fish on it. It lay there on its side, staring back at her with its one congealed eye.

Wahoo! Karen Keable said.

Rachel jumped.

What?

The local fish. Wahoo. You'll never taste anything as fresh. They whip them out of the water and bring them straight to the table. That fish was probably alive and swimming in the bay less than ten minutes ago.

Rachel pushed back her chair and stood up. Felt her napkin drift to the floor. Karen Keable was looking at her with a mouthful of fish.

Are you all right? You're not feeling faint again, are you?

She tried to smile, feeling around for her bag.

I'm fine, she said. Just popping to the loo.

She stood there for a moment, looking around for an escape route. The restaurant had been quiet when they came in, but now it was thick and full – chairs, people, everything.

And then suddenly there she was. The sad girl with the big teeth and worried face.

You want the rest room?

Rachel stared at her for a moment. She nodded.

She followed the girl across the room. They twisted easily between the chairs. Past some loud men. Then down some steps. Past potted plants and along a short corridor. Then some more steps.

The rest room had an old-fashioned sign with a picture of a lady on it. Rachel pushed the door and turned to thank the girl, expecting her to go. But she followed her in.

They stared at each other in the sudden silence.

The room was painted fleshy pink, with a large upholstered chair. A long table with a mirror and a couple of fancy chandelier lights over it. A white orchid in a pot. A box of tissues.

She sank down in the chair. Peace and quiet. She put her hand on the place where the baby was.

Thank you, she told the girl. Thank you so much.

The girl still stood there and Rachel wondered if she was expecting a tip. Then she took a breath as if she was about to cry.

What is it? Rachel said. What's the matter?

The girl could not look at her. She wore a small silver cross around her neck and she fingered it now, twisting it nervously back and forth.

It's your husband, she said.

Rachel felt herself flush.

What do you mean? What about him?

The girl moved closer. She bent close enough that Rachel could smell her slightly sour, young breath.

You must tell him to leave. He must go now. If he stays here, he is in very great danger. He —

Rachel stared at her.

But how could he be in danger? What kind of danger?

The girl closed her eyes. Her mouth twisted.

I can't say it. Please. I don't want to say it.

Rachel felt herself tense.

But you don't even know my husband.

He is upstairs, yes? The man in the red shirt? Curly brown hair? Talking all the time?

Rachel nodded. That was Dan.

Tears were standing in the girl's eyes.

Make him go, she said. Please. I am asking you — nice lady with baby — I am very afraid —

Rachel felt her heart speed up.

How do you know that? How do you know that I'm having a baby?

The girl didn't look at her. She put her face in her hands and she burst into tears. Rachel stood up. The girl was sobbing. Rachel glanced across at the box of tissues.

Hortensia, she said as she reached across to pull one from the box. Please, I don't understand. You have to tell me what you mean, what exactly it is that you're —

As her fingers touched the tissue box, there was a creaking sound. Followed by a loud wrenching, the sound of something cracking and tearing —

They both stopped, eyes on each other.

The chandelier lights over the mirror flickered, went out, came on again. She saw the girl's face. Watched her begin to back away, breathing hard, feeling around for the door handle.

No! Rachel shouted. Stay!

The voice was not her own. The girl froze and began to cry. And they both watched as, very slowly but deftly, as if some unseen hand had taken a tool to them, the dozen or more small steel screws which held the lights to the wall began to twist, turn, unwind, slow at first, then faster, faster.

One by one they flew from their fixings, skittering off in all directions, bouncing along the dressing table onto the floor. Then, instead of falling straight down to the table below, the lights themselves were hurled through the air and dashed themselves against the wall opposite.

*

She got herself upstairs. The air was black. Her skin was cold, her mouth dry. Dan was still talking to the couple, a cigarette in one hand, lighter in the other, the wine bottle empty in front of him. He broke off to look at her upset face.

What now? he said.

Before she could speak, he pulled her onto his lap. Kissed the side of her head. She smelled his boozy breath.

You're freezing, he said. You're like ice. Come here, wifey, I'll warm you up.

He took her hands in his and rubbed them. She didn't resist. She still said nothing. Her teeth banging in her head.

Rachel, he said. This is Shelley. Shelley and Mick.

Hey, said Mick.

Shelley looked at Rachel and smiled.

He's been telling us all about his book, Mick said.

Boring them stupid, Dan said.

Rachel was confused.

What book? He hasn't written a book.

Dan laughed.

The one I want to write, darling. The one I'm going to write, remember? Mick's brother's a publisher. He does the Late-Late series. Didn't you read one of them once? I'm sure you did. Something about fish —

35

The Fish Bowl? Shelley said.

That's right. *The Fish Bowl* – remember? You said you liked it. And that thing about the man who swam the Channel with no legs, remember that? They made it into a film.

Rachel shivered. She couldn't remember anything about a fish or a man with no legs. She reached over and tried to pick up Dan's water glass but her hands were shaking too much. She felt Shelley looking at her.

Are you OK? she said.

She picked up the glass and passed it to Rachel. Rachel sipped at it. She felt herself begin to cry. Suddenly afraid of the glass, she put it back down.

Darling, Dan said. For goodness' sake –

Shelley leaned over and rubbed at her shoulder.

Look at you, you poor thing. You're in a real state. What's the matter?

Her fingers were hot and moist. Rachel tried to pull away. She shut her eyes.

Something horrible –

What? Shelley said.

Just now, in the Ladies. The lights – they just came right off the wall.

Mick let out a breath and shook his head.

This place, he said. Do you know, Shelley went to

take a shower and the shower head thingy just came away in her hands?

Plaster and crap and stuff all over my feet, Shelley said. It was unbelievable. We'd only just unpacked and we had to move rooms.

They didn't even apologise, Mick said.

Well, they did, Shelley said.

Not properly. Not as if they meant it.

Shelley picked up her wine glass, glancing at Dan.

It's true, she said. They weren't that good about it.

I'm not going to let it go, Mick said. I'm bashing out a letter as soon as we get home —

No, Rachel said, interrupting him. It wasn't like that. I mean, it wasn't an accident.

You what? Mick said. He picked up his glass. Drained it.

Rachel looked at Dan.

It was intended, she said.

Intended?

Dan began to smile. Shelley caught his eye and made a face. Rachel ignored her.

It was exactly like what happened earlier. With the glass, on the terrace. Seriously, Dan. It wasn't me. It just happened. As if someone had done it.

Shelley looked interested.

What happened on the terrace?

Nothing, Dan said. It really wasn't anything.

He pulled up a chair and shifted Rachel off his lap.

Seriously, Shelley said. Tell me.

Rachel didn't look at her. She really did wish she'd shut up.

Nothing, she said. He's right. It's not important.

Dan was smiling.

And anyway, my love, let's be rational for a moment. What do both incidents have in common?

She stared at him.

What? You honestly think I'd make this up? Or — you think it was me — that I did it?

He shrugged.

I'm not saying anything. I'm seeing if there's any chance of another bottle of this excellent whatever it's called —

He held up the bottle and a waitress came. Before Rachel could say anything else, Shelley leaned forward, touched her wrist.

Don't worry, she said. I'm sure there'll be an explanation. There always is. I always imagine all sorts of things when I'm tired.

And by the way, she added, I think we have a friend in common. Had. We knew Rufus Robinson. We only met him once or twice. But Tash is a very good friend of my sister's. And I hear he was a really close friend of yours. I'm so sorry. It must have been a terrible shock.

Rachel caught her breath. For a second or two, she struggled to think.

He was Dan's friend really, she said. I mean, I knew him of course but – he and Dan went way back. They were at school together.

She looked at Dan. He stared at the table. They were all silent for a moment.

Such bloody awful timing, too, Mick said. Isn't she about to give birth or something?

Rachel swallowed, wishing this hadn't all come up now. She didn't want to have to think about Natasha or Rufus or any of it –

She's having twins, she said. In April. They'd been trying for ages.

It was a bit of a sore point actually, Dan said. They'd had about eight million rounds of IVF and then we go and get up the duff by accident.

Mick looked at him and made a face.

By accident?

Dan, Rachel said. Please. You're drunk.

Shelley looked at Rachel.

I'm sure it was a very happy accident, she said.

Rachel said nothing. Remembering Dan's face when she told him. The afternoon of shouting and tears which followed.

Shelley sighed.

And he was such an amazing actor, wasn't he? What was that thing with Colin Firth? I loved him in that.

Dan lit a cigarette, batting the smoke away from Rachel.

He wasn't amazing. He was fucking terrible. A fucking terrible actor. And that thing with Colin Firth was about fifteen years ago, straight after university. You wouldn't know it from the way he went on about it, but he'd done almost nothing since –

Mick and Shelley stared at him.

But I thought he'd had this big break? Shelley said. Just before he died. Hadn't he just done some great big detective thing on TV?

Dan shrugged and sucked on his cigarette.

A piece of crap, that's what it was.

Dan, Rachel said again.

The bottle came and he poured more wine, filling the glasses a little too full. He looked at Shelley. Rachel recognised his drunk-angry-not-letting-go face and her heart sank.

I tell you, he was lousy. Rufus was lousy. It was all talk. He should have given up long ago and done something worthwhile with his life.

Rachel looked at him.

Stop it, she said. I mean it. You'll regret this later.

Dan blew out smoke.

I don't know why you care, he said. You never liked him much anyway.

Rachel hesitated for a moment. She looked at Shelley.

It's not true, she said. None of it's true. Don't listen to him. I don't know what's got into him.

Shelley smiled.

It's OK, she said. We understand. Seriously. Chill.

Dan stubbed out his cigarette. He stared at the stub and for a moment he looked as if he might cry.

We were best mates, he said. We knew each other since we were seven. I loved the guy. But it doesn't mean I can't criticise him, does it?

They went for a walk on the beach. Rachel said she was tired, but Dan insisted.

It's too dark, she said.

She was still shaky and cold. The sky was thick and black, shadows everywhere. She kept on having to look around her. Dan made a face.

Too dark? It's perfect. Just us and the moonlight. It's the first night of our honeymoon. Come on, darling. It's practically obligatory.

The first night of our honeymoon and you're completely drunk, she said as they waved goodbye to the others and went down the steps and onto the wooden walkway that led to the beach.

I'm not drunk.

You didn't have to be so mean about Rufus either, she said.

He stopped and felt around in his pockets. She knew he was searching for his cigarettes. He found them.

I loved the man, you know I did. But I'm not going to put him up on some pedestal just because he's dead. Apart from anything else, he wouldn't want me to. Anyway, he said, lighting his cigarette. That dinner was so boring. And I was pining for you. There was nothing to do but drink.

She thought of saying that he could easily have insisted on sitting with her. But she didn't. Instead she told him how Karen Keable had managed to find out that they were on their honeymoon.

Dan laughed and sucked hard on the cigarette. He laced the fingers of his other hand with hers.

Does it matter? he said.

But she'll be going on about it, whenever we run into her. We'll never hear the end of it now.

Fuck's sake, he said. Can we please have a ban on talking about the Keables? There's only one thing I'm finding more excruciating than having to talk to the woman. And that's having to listen to you talking about talking to her.

Rachel laughed. Then she couldn't resist telling him about Cedric's honeymoon packages.

We could have had Action, Romance or Indulgence, she said.

Or sex? Dan said. Was there a sex package?

She looked at him.

You've already got the sex package.

He turned her towards him.

I love you, Rach.

She sighed.

I love you too.

I'm sorry I was mean to you earlier.

You weren't mean.

I was, he said. You know I was. I'm sorry I couldn't take it seriously when the lights fell off the wall in the ladies' room or whatever.

He began to laugh and she let him.

They came to the end of the walkway and kicked off their shoes and felt the sand – surprisingly cold – under their feet. The air was still warm but heavy and damp.

Is it the dew? she said, looking around her.

What? – he was stumbling a little – Is what the dew?

The damp. Do you think there's a dew already?

He put his arm around her.

I don't know what you're talking about, he said.

You can't feel it?

No.

She looked around her again. Everything was black and cold.

I wish we were at home, she said.

Dan laughed.

You're not serious.

She was serious. She thought of the cup of tea drunk standing in the cold kitchen while he checked their tickets and passports. Had it really only been that morning? She thought of Tigger, probably sitting hunched on the kitchen counter, waiting for the neighbour to come in and feed him.

No, she said. Of course I'm not.

He squeezed her hand and she squeezed back

and the moon came out from behind the clouds. Bright now, silvery, slicing its beams down into the water.

She glanced back at their shoes, lying in the sand at the edge of the jetty.

Aren't you worried? she asked him. About what the driver said?

He thought about it. Blew out smoke.

No, he said. I'm not worried. Next question.

She looked at him.

You don't think it's at all weird?

He shrugged.

People say funny things. So what?

She took a breath. Hortensia's sad anxious face came into her head.

This place, she said.

What about it?

I don't know.

He threw down his cigarette. Held out his arms.

Come here, he said.

Why?

Just do it.

He grabbed her hand, pulled her back away from the water and steered her up the beach, pushing her deep into the shadows and down into the sand. Pushing her down a little too roughly, pushing up her skirt, scraping at her knickers. She felt cold on her back. And damp.

What? she said, half laughing, half struggling. What are you doing?

What do you think I'm doing?

It was over in seconds. They held on to each other. Her legs were shaking. She pushed him off so she could check there was no one around. There wasn't.

She lifted her hips to pull up her knickers, pull down her dress. When she'd finished, he put his head back down on her. She touched his hair. Her cheeks were burning.

Hot, he said. Hot pregnant lady.

Her heart was banging. She lay back and watched the sky. It didn't look that dark from here – dull and blueish and drained of light. Fast-moving shadows, blotting out the moon.

Clouds, she said.

What?

I saw them earlier. I don't want clouds. I hope they won't be here tomorrow.

Dan pushed her hair from her face. He did it so gently that it tickled.

They won't be here, he said.

How do you know?

I know everything, he said.

*

He'd said they were going to go and look at the tree frogs on the way back. They were supposed to be amazing, he said. Clinging to a vine on the wall by the gym block. A noise like nothing you'd ever heard. Mick and Shelley had discovered them on the way to dinner and told him where to find them.

I hope we're not going to have to be with them all the time, Rachel said.

What? The tree frogs?

No, Mick and Shelley. You seem to be such great pals already.

Dan stopped to light another cigarette. She knew that he thought he was getting away with it, smoking so much, when he was supposed to be cutting down. What had happened to the deal they had, that he would have stopped by the time the baby came?

Look, he said. Mick's brother's that guy I told you about. The publisher who everyone says is so hot. And I'm going to need someone to sell my book to –

But you haven't written your book. You haven't written a word of it. It doesn't exist. It's just an idea you had one time when you were –

She was going to say drunk, but she stopped herself. He looked at her. His eyes were cold.

Thanks, he said. Thanks for the vote of confidence.

I didn't mean it like that.

He was silent a moment.

All I'm saying is it's a contact, isn't it? And it's quite a coincidence, meeting Mick. Come on, Rach. It's a break. What am I going to do when they drop my column? I need a break, don't I?

She said nothing. And even though she tried not to let him, Rufus came into her head. Rufus and his big, wonderful break. They'd all gone out to dinner at Sheekey's when he heard – a joke because he and Dan had once been waiters there. Not even waiters. Washer-uppers. And now it was lobster and champagne, on him. The first of many, Rufus had said. He'd made sure to give the waiter and the coat girl generous tips. He'd have given one to the washer-upper too, if he could have.

She shivered, shaking herself free of the thought.

They were going to take a detour to look at the frogs but by the time they got back to the block where their room was, Rachel realised Dan had forgotten all about it. She didn't care. In fact she was glad. All she could think of was that great big bed with its rattan headboard and clean, cool white sheets.

The room had been done. They'd drawn the curtains, turned back the bed, folding the sheets into neat corners. They'd lined up all her bottles in rows.

Annoyingly, they'd found the bedspread and cushions that she'd stowed at the top of the wardrobe and replaced them on the bed.

She picked them up in one armful and hurled them across the room. They narrowly missed a glass, but caught at Dan's headphones which were on the edge of the coffee table and knocked them onto the floor.

Hey, he said. Steady on.

He picked up his precious headphones, wound the wire around them. She felt him looking at her.

And you're telling me that the glass just picked itself up and threw itself?

She said nothing.

The person who did the room had also put the air-con on. It was much too cold. It took Dan a minute or two to work out how to turn it off and by the time he'd done it, she was almost asleep.

The last thing she heard him say was tree frogs.

What?

I didn't show you the tree frogs, he said.

Chapter Two

Next morning she woke early and slid out of bed without waking him. She picked up her swimsuit, pulled it on in the bathroom, twisted her hair up and, grabbing the first towel that came to hand, opened the bedroom door as quietly as she could and released herself, barefoot and grateful, into the sunshine.

Their room had been in shadow. But out here, the air was bursting with brightness. She smelled flowers. Warm early light on stone. Birds were calling. Bees drifting and dipping among the vines and creepers. Acacia, mangrove, bougainvillea —

A dozen steps brought her down to the little pool. Half of it still plunged in shadow, the other half already bright with sun. Spots of light wobbling around on the blue water. She had to shield her eyes.

Next to the pool was a bar. A used beer glass had a wasp crawling inside it.

Not a soul anywhere in sight. Far away she heard the drone of a lawnmower.

She draped her towel over the back of a chair, but realised that the chair was wet, so she took it off and spread it on the already warm stones. A couple of curled brown leaves floated on the surface of the pool. She put her legs in the water. She knew it would be freezing and it was. She sat for a moment, letting herself get used to it, leaning back on her hands, looking around her, the sun already hot on her shoulders.

With every second that passed, the water grew warmer. She dipped her hand and wetted herself. Then, shivering, she took a breath and tipped herself in.

She came up exhilarated, gasping.

It was there. Standing on the white concrete path which wound from the pool up towards reception. Watching her. It had a face, eyes, greyish clothes, a shock of black hair. Human shape.

For a moment, all colour drained from the air. The heat, the light, the distant sound of the mower — everything stopped. She froze. She could not breathe. Weighed down by darkness and sadness. She wanted to look away but she could not. It wanted her to be fixed on it. It wanted her to see. For a quick, terrible second, their eyes met —

Then, as she watched, it turned away and continued on up the slope, its dark shape shifting and smudging until finally it let itself dissolve to nothing among the shadows beneath the trees.

They breakfasted late, in the Rainbow Garden — an airy, open space under a bamboo awning, with a patio that snaked all the way around.

They found a table in the furthest corner. A smiling waitress came and poured coffee. She asked for their room number and Dan showed her their key. Still beaming, she wrote it down.

Rachel put her sunglasses down on the table and poured herself some iced water from a metal jug. She looked around to see if she could see Hortensia. She couldn't. Dan was putting milk in his coffee.

So, he said. What now?

I think you go and help yourself, she said.

Go on, then.

I'm not very hungry.

He gave her a look.

How's our baby going to grow if you don't eat?

He was right. She went over to look at the buffet.

There were warm meats with greyish veins in them. Cooked mushrooms, black and slippery. An egg, solidifying as it cooled.

On the other side of the table, pale-faced people in shorts and sandals queued for omelettes. Dreading catching sight of Karen Keable, or even Mick and Shelley, she turned away.

She got herself some fruit. Mango. Papaya. Pineapple. A small pot of yoghourt which she knew she wouldn't eat.

Dan went up and came back with a croissant. Two slices of cheese. A waffle. Some strawberries. And a runny mess which seemed to be undercooked scrambled eggs. Rachel tried not to look at the eggs. Dan broke off a piece of croissant and crumbs sprayed. Immediately two small brown sparrows came swooping down.

Cheeky buggers!

He shooed them away but they only perched on the next table, watching him. Beady black eyes, cocked heads. After a moment, they swooped again.

Jesus, he said. It's like something out of bloody Hitchcock.

Rachel was laughing. He looked at her.

That's nice.

What's nice?

To see you laughing. I don't think you've cracked a smile since we got here.

That's not true, she said.

It is, he said. It is true.

She said nothing.

He buttered a piece of croissant, pushed some scrambled egg onto it and put it in his mouth. Chewing, he placed a hand on her knee.

Come on, he said. You've got to eat.

She picked up her fork, looked at the fruit. All those vitamins. She knew it would do her baby good. She picked up her knife and fork and cut a piece of papaya. The blade slid easily through. She lifted it to her mouth and bit on it —

Flesh. Crimson juice exploding in her mouth. The oily metallic tang of blood —

She spat the whole thing out. There was a hush. One or two heads turning.

Dan bent towards her, gripped her arm.

What the hell — are you OK?

Quickly, she drank some water. Held a napkin to her mouth. Tried to swallow. The taste of blood was still there. She took another sip, tried not to retch.

Is it bad? he said. If it's bad we'll send it back —

He pushed his chair back and looked around for a waiter.

Dan, she said and he looked at her. Please don't.

He shook his head.

Look, he said. This place isn't cheap.

She swallowed. When he looked at her again, his eyes were calm. He took her hand, squeezed it.

Maybe it's a pregnancy thing, he said. Like the sickness?

She nodded. She hadn't really had any sickness.

Maybe, she said.

By the time they got to the beach, nearly all of the umbrellas were taken. Even the empty ones had towels or swimsuits firmly draped over them. They investigated the strip of sand further off, but Rachel saw that the water there was full of seaweed. There seemed to be a free umbrella with a couple of loungers, but when they got closer they saw that both seats were collapsed and broken.

Not good enough, Dan said. It really isn't. I'm going to say something to Cedric about this.

Or do the same as Mick, Rachel said. Fire off a nice long letter of complaint as soon as you get home.

Dan looked at her for a second. Then he saw that she was joking and he laughed.

They settled themselves near some palm trees, further back from the water.

It was already nearly midday, the sun fierce and hot. Rachel could feel her shoulders starting to burn. She kicked off her sandals and immediately the sand scorched her feet. Yelping, she stepped back into the shade of the umbrella. Dug around in her bag for the sunscreen.

Dan was spreading his towel on his lounger, taking care to make sure the corners were just so. Rachel smiled. When he'd finished, he stood frowning and looking around, up and down the beach.

You don't mind? he said. That we can smell that?

He indicated the little thatched bar further down, where they were already frying fish and something else – was it burgers?

Rachel, pulling off her sundress and hanging it by its straps on a hook on the umbrella, shook her head.

It's fine. It's quite nice, actually.

She settled herself on her lounger.

Ah, he said. Not so nauseous after all.

He peeled off his clothes so he was down to his trunks and continued to look around him, squinting into the sun and scratching himself.

Rachel shaded her eyes and looked at him.

What is it? What are you looking for?

He glanced down at her.

Nothing, he said. Just looking. Just taking it all in.

Isn't it glorious? she said.

It's paradise.

She took off her sunglasses and reached up and wiped them on the edge of her sundress. Put them back on. Looked at him again, standing over her.

What? he said.

She tried to smile.

Nothing. You're blocking my sun, that's all.

He stepped away. Took off his watch, his sunglasses.

I'm going straight in, he said. Wanna come?

She looked out at the water.

I think I'll wait, she told him. I just want to lie here and read my book.

He didn't try to make her change her mind. She watched as he jogged off down the sand, away from her.

At the edge of the water, a young woman in a bikini, maybe an au pair, sat cross-legged, playing with a small fair-haired child. The child was naked apart from a sunhat and water wings. She watched as Dan, wading straight in, turned and said something to the girl. As if in answer, the child raised its spade in the air and Dan pretended to fall backwards, into the water.

He pushed off, laughing, on his back. So at ease, she thought. At ease with everybody, always expecting to be liked. It was a quality that Rufus had shared. A complete lack of anxiety. A sense of ease and entitlement.

She picked up her book. She hadn't looked at it since the plane and just opening it now brought it all back to her. The cramped seats and scrunched-up blankets. The queue for the toilets. The disappointing Woody Allen film. And the sight of her new wedding ring, bright and unlikely in the white beam of the reading light, as Dan slept beside her.

She shook the thought away and frowned, turning the pages, trying to remember where she'd got to.

Something made her look up. She shaded her eyes and scanned the edges of the water. The girl and child had gone. No sign of Dan either. The beach was emptying. Lunchtime. She wondered if she was hungry.

A boy came by, pushing a cart with cold drinks.

Coca-Cola? he said. Soda? Beer? Rum? Fruit punch?

She smiled and shook her head and then, the moment he moved away, regretted it. She was thirsty. Why hadn't she asked him for water?

She went back to her book. Found the place again. She was just sinking back in, trying to turn the words into something more than words, when she felt it —

A hush. A deadening.

She caught her breath and looked up. It was there. No more than a few feet away, making its slow way along the dirt path which led to the bar. She gazed at its odd, persuasively human shape — pale face, black hair, a man or a boy, male anyway. And it had put on city clothes. Some kind of a suit. Thick fabric, at odds with the beach.

She stared, keeping her eyes on the back of it, waiting to see if it would stop at the bar. But no, it continued on round the corner, towards the dusty white space that was the car park.

As it disappeared out of sight, she realised she'd got herself up off the lounger and was standing in bright sunshine, her face tipped up towards the sky and her book dropped in the sand.

Dan came back up the beach. Smiling, dripping. He grabbed the towel off the lounger, rubbed at his hair.

Don't you think you should be in the shade? he said. You'll burn if you stay there like that.

I am burning, she said.

He stared at her.

Then — for fuck's sake. What are you doing? Get back under the umbrella.

She looked down at her burning skin. She had no idea why she'd put herself there. All she knew was that as soon as the feeling of what she'd seen had left her, she'd spread her towel on the sand and lain down flat in the scorching midday sunshine and stayed there, feeling the lick and bite of it on her skin. Hotter and hotter. Burning. She hadn't moved once for the next ten minutes except to brush a fly off her leg.

Now she did as he told her. Got up off the sand and put herself back in the shade of the umbrella. He was still staring at her.

Seriously, my sweet, I don't understand. Look at you — look at your face. What on earth did you think you were doing?

She shrugged, trying to smile at him.

I wanted to warm up.

He stood looking at her for a moment, still damp all over from the sea. She had no idea what he was thinking. At last he tossed the towel on the lounger, looked up at the sky.

Well, next time don't do it at this time of day. And maybe go in the sea first to cool down. That water, it's just — it's —

Rachel squinted at him.

Is it perfection? she said. Is this paradise?

He hesitated, watching her again.

You're in a very strange mood, he said.

She smiled.

What is it? he said. What's the matter? Seriously, Rach. Are you OK?

She didn't answer him. She couldn't. She didn't even know the answer herself. She picked her book up, shook the sand from its pages.

That was a very long swim, she said.

He didn't look at her.

Yes, well, I decided to strike out.

Everyone's gone for lunch, she said.

He picked up his watch, looked at it as he put it on.

And that's exactly where we're going in just a minute. Rosi's is the place.

Rosi's?

It's right on the other side, beyond the main building. High up in the trees. View of the Atlantic instead of the bay. Completely different from here. You'll be amazed.

Rachel shoved her book in her bag and reached up for her sundress.

How do you know? she said.

What?

How do you know what the view's like?

He ran his fingers through his hair. He made a face.
I told you. I know everything.

They ate wahoo and salad at a wooden table in a restaurant high up in the trees with a view over the wide, crashing Atlantic ocean. It was late and they'd almost stopped serving. Just a few stragglers finishing their coffee, one or two kids running up and down.

The breeze blew her hair into her eyes. Dan ordered a beer.

My god, he said. Have you seen yourself?

Her hand flew to her face.

Am I burnt?

That's putting it mildly. Take a look at your nose and forehead. You need to put something on that, my sweet.

She pulled out her compact. He was still shaking his head.

What on earth did you think you were doing? It's not like you. You're usually the one telling me to put more cream on.

It was true. She was always so careful about the sun. Her mum had the complexion of a person half her age – years of wide-brimmed hats and factor 30. She liked to think she took after her mum.

She snapped the compact shut and dropped it in her bag.

I'll put something on it when we get back to the room, she said.

He stabbed a potato with his fork.

Just don't complain later, he said. When I tell you to get all dolled up so I can take you out for a lobster dinner.

She glanced at him in surprise and he grinned.

You know the smart restaurant up by the spa? Riccardo's, I think it's called. Cedric said it was worth booking, so I did. Eight o'clock. Oh, and before you ask, I looked in the book and checked that no one had written the name 'Keable' anywhere on the page.

She smiled and took his hand, kissed the warm tips of his fingers.

I hope there is lobster.

He rolled his eyes.

You think I'd have booked without checking? Hey, I've worked out what these strange, smooth potatoes remind me of. Do you remember Yeoman's tinned potatoes? Oh no, of course you don't, you're much too posh.

She looked at the potato on his fork.

I'm not posh, she said.

He made a sign to the waiter that he'd like another beer.

Come on. All I'm saying is you had the staff.

Rachel thought about her father. How he didn't even like having nurses around the house, let alone cooks.

My father wasn't like that, she said. He didn't like having people wait on him. There was this one guy who ran the estate, and I think his son helped him out sometimes. Apart from that, well, I suppose there was just the nurse.

She said nurse. But actually it was lots of nurses, from an agency. Looking after a paralysed man was a 24-hour job, so they rotated. Some were better than others. Her mother could be reduced to tears by a bad one.

Dan's beer arrived. He looked at it, silent for a moment.

I wish I'd known him, he said.

Rachel said nothing. She'd met Dan just a week or so after her father died. Just when she was at her very lowest. Terrible or wonderful timing, depending on how you looked at it. She barely knew him, but somehow he had been there. By the time she looked up again, ready to face the world, they seemed to be a couple.

64

He looked at her.

I wasn't meaning to be unkind about him, you know.

I know, she said. I know you weren't.

A tiny starved-looking cat was winding herself around Dan's legs. He dropped some fish for her. Immediately, three skinny grey kittens appeared. Rachel watched as he threw a bit of fish towards them. She held her breath —

Shh, Dan said.

They all miaowed loudly. The biggest one started to creep towards the fish, its tail stiffly pointing. It had almost reached it when Rachel's chair scraped loudly backwards on the wooden decking. The kitten skittered away.

Dan groaned.

What did you have to go and do that for?

He picked up another bit of fish.

Now we've got to start all over again, he said.

She froze, staring at him. Then she stood up, took a step away from the chair. Her heart was in her throat.

I didn't, she said.

What?

Dan, I didn't do it. The chair —

He shook his head.

Oh for god's sake, Rach. Please. Don't go starting all of that again.

He threw more fish. The boldest kitten miaowed soundlessly and began to creep forward.

Poor little thing, he said. I bet you're bloody sick of wahoo, aren't you? And you have my full sympathy.

Rachel stood there for a moment. She looked at the chair. It stayed where it was. She went over and sat on the other one, on the other side of the table. She put her head in her hands.

Dan wiped his fingers on the napkin.

So — what? You're trying to tell me that the chair moved by itself?

She shook her head. Looked up and away, out at the sea. White and foamy, waves crashing. She swallowed.

You can't feel it, can you? she said. You've no idea —

He looked at her. A careful look. She could see he was trying to decide what to say. She shook her head. She wanted to cry.

You can't feel it? The thing that's here. It's just me, isn't it?

He put a hand on her arm. He was smiling now.

My darling, he began.

She waited for him to say something else, but he didn't. He squeezed her arm.

She said nothing. Looking down, she saw the grainy wood of the table, between the slats the crumb-strewn floor.

I can't stay here, she whispered. There's something terrible in this place. I can't stay here.

He took her back to the room and made her get into bed.

I'm not saying I won't listen. But I refuse to talk seriously about giving up on our one and only honeymoon until you've had a proper rest.

She told him she wasn't tired. He stroked her head.

Darling, the first trimester is supposed to be the hardest. All those cells dividing and dividing. I don't think you realise. You're incredibly raw.

She told him she wasn't in the first trimester. Fourteen weeks was the second trimester. And anyway it was nothing to do with the cells. Her baby's cells. It was nothing to do with the baby. In fact she wanted the baby kept out of it.

Don't leave me, she said. Don't go anywhere. I mean it, Dan. I don't want to be left alone in this room.

She looked around her, suddenly afraid of every - thing – the gleaming furniture, the pictures, the great big bed with its shiny bedspread and perfect, sharp corners. Even their own familiar belongings strewn around.

I won't even think about leaving you, he said. I'm staying right here. Look, here I am.

He lay down beside her and put a hand exactly where she liked it, ever so gently gripping the hot, damp nape of her neck.

When she woke, she did feel calmer. She opened her eyes to see him crouching on the floor by the fridge. He pushed the door closed.

At least that's been restocked, he said.

He pulled up the blind. Afternoon sunlight crept around, eating up the room. There were two bananas on a plate, a knife and napkin beside them. He took one and, peeling it, walked out onto the terrace.

Don't move, he said. Don't do anything. You lie there and wake up as slowly as you like.

She shut her eyes, hoping to drift back to sleep again, but she knew she couldn't. The pillow was hot. Her face on fire. She touched her cheeks and, remembering, rolled out of bed and went into the bathroom.

She pulled off her sundress and her swimsuit and splashed her hands and face with cold water. She put cream all over. She tried not to look in the mirror, but she saw there was an angry red line across the top of her breasts where her swimsuit had been.

She put on one of the white towelling robes, knotting it around her waist. When she went back in the room, Dan was lying on the bed holding a piece of paper. He waved it at her.

We have to do this. Sunset cocktails at Shirley Heights. It's tonight.

Shirley who? Rachel said.

She went over to the fridge to get a bottle of water. Dan laughed.

Not Shirley Who. Shirley Heights. It's a place, not a person. Supposed to be an amazing view. People go there to watch the sun go down.

Rachel poured a glass of water and slid back into bed.

Do we have to? she said.

Dan picked up the remote, pointed it at the TV. It crackled into life.

We don't have to. Of course we don't have to. But it might be fun. Don't worry, we won't talk to anyone. We'll just go there and get a drink and stick together and watch the sun go down.

He looked at her.

It's romantic.

Yeah, she said.

What? He kept his eyes on the TV. You don't want to? You're still thinking you want to get the first plane out of here?

Rachel looked at him. There were tears in her throat but she swallowed them back.

Am I going mad? she said.

He laughed and ruffled her hair.

Silly girl. Of course you're not going mad. Don't be ridiculous. You're just in a funny old state, that's all.

She swallowed.

You don't believe me, do you? You don't believe a single thing I've told you.

He shrugged.

It's not a question of believing or not believing —

What then?

For a moment, he looked as if he was going to say something. Then he shook his head, looked back at the TV.

All I know for sure is that you need to try and relax. Stop rushing at everything. Slow down. Take some breaths. Give it a few days and then we'll see.

A few days? She thought about the glass, the lights, the chair. A shock of black hair, pale skin, greyish clothes. She shivered and shook the thought away.

But what if I'm not mad? she said. What if there really is something bad here?

Dan was zapping through the TV channels. For a few seconds they both watched something that looked like a French game show. A tall blonde woman in a swimsuit held a card with a number on it. The screen exploded with stars.

Look, he said. If Cedric turns out to be a serial killer with a thing for honeymoon couples, then I think we should get the hell out of here. But if we're just talking a bit of superstitious voodoo nonsense from people who don't know any better, then I think I'd be inclined to shrug it off and get on with enjoying my holiday.

He turned back to the screen and went on flicking through the channels till he found some cricket.

A few minutes later, though, rolling onto her stomach to feel around for her pregnancy bible which had somehow ended up under the bed, Rachel made a noise of surprise. She slid her hand under her belly and waited, holding her breath.

What? Dan said.

His eyes didn't leave the TV.

It moved.

What?

The baby. Just now. I felt it move. It was amazing. Like a little bubble bursting inside me. Here —

What?

Give me your hand. I want you to feel it.

He let his hand be taken. She slid it under her belly, just below her navel. Waited.

Well? she said.

Well what?

Can you feel it?

No, he said.

No?

I don't think so, no.

He pulled his hand away, his eyes still on the cricket.

You don't want to feel it?

Don't be silly. Of course I do.

Here then —

She reached out for his hand and he gave it back to her and she put it there again, but of course nothing happened. It was over. The magic had gone. She pushed his hand away.

Isn't it a bit early anyway? he said after a moment or two.

Early?

For the baby to be moving?

She looked at him sitting there, his mouth slack, his eyes on the screen.

No, she said, curling away from him and putting her hand back on the place. It's not too early. It's exactly the right time.

The drive to Shirley Heights took fifteen minutes. After a steep climb, the bus stopped in a cloud of dust and people unbelted and doors slid open. They found themselves in a hot, unshaded car-parking area, next to a gift shop.

A dreadlocked man in a rasta hat had maracas and tambourines and little steel drums spread out for sale on a bright-coloured sheet. Small children raced around. From beyond the shop Rachel heard the lazy bump of reggae music, the smell of barbecue and smoke, the roar of voices.

Even though Dan had promised they wouldn't, they got stuck with Mick and Shelley. She would just have walked away but she knew he wouldn't dream of it. He squeezed her hand by way of apology. She didn't squeeze back.

So how long till it actually goes down? Mick said.

God knows, Dan said. But you can be sure they'll spin it out, so they can take our money from us for as long as possible.

There's supposed to be a green flash, Shelley said.

A what? said Mick.

At the very last minute, just before the sun goes. A bright green flash or something. It's to do with the light.

She turned and looked at Rachel.

Wow. Look at you. You caught the sun.

Yes, Rachel said. I know.

They all stood around for a moment without saying anything.

We should go through, Dan said at last. I don't think this is going to be bearable without at least a few beers.

They went through. Instantly, the noise and heat increased. Smoke billowed from the brick barbecue. A crowd of people queuing with paper plates.

Mick and Dan went to get drinks and Shelley went to find the toilets. Glad to be left alone, Rachel made her way over to the low grey stone wall which looked down over English Harbour. She wasn't in the mood to be impressed, but it was impressive. The drop was dramatic. You could see for miles.

Like standing on the edge of the world, isn't it?

A man in a leather cowboy hat was grinning at her. She nodded.

Where you from, then? he said.

She smiled and eased herself away, weaving through the crowd till she found another gap where she could push through and look out again.

The sky was still a violent blue, but the light was leaving it fast. Sun spilled across the horizon, turning everything bright gold. Down below in the harbour, a clutter of boats already lay in darkness.

The crowd was thick and excited. Somewhere someone lit a joint and its sweet, herby odour filled the air. A man coughed and spat. A woman laughed and called to someone. Couples kissed and broke apart and kissed again. A man with a child balanced on his shoulders used his free hand to point to the sun.

Watch that. It'll be gone in a minute.

Why? shouted the child. Gone where?

Laughter sank through the crowd. The smoke from the barbecue drifted over. It got in Rachel's throat and made her eyes water. She felt the black, mineral taste of dirt rise into her mouth –

It was there. He was there. Coming closer.

She couldn't do anything. She wanted to cry out, to move away, but she couldn't. Everything was stopped

— she couldn't think or breathe or speak. Just before she shut her eyes, she heard a strangled, smothered voice and she knew the voice was hers and that she had to get herself out of his reach somehow, but it was already too late. The distance between them had hardened, tightened — nothing to separate them now. She heard him speak.

Hamilton, he said.

She felt his hand closing, cold and waxen, around hers. She saw teeth. She thought he might be smiling.

I think we're staying at the same resort, he said.

She screamed.

She was sitting on the wall. Dan was holding her. One arm around her shoulders, the other around her waist.

It's all my fault, he said. I'm so sorry, darling. I'm an idiot. I shouldn't have left you for so long. The bar was bloody ridiculous —

We were queuing for fucking ages, Mick said. We sent Shelley off to look for you.

Shelley's face came close.

Rachel, where were you? I looked everywhere. I thought you were in the loo. What happened? Are you OK?

Dan made her sip some water. The sky was dark.

The reggae had stopped and a steel band was playing.

This low blood pressure of yours, he said. You were lucky you didn't fall and hurt yourself.

What if she'd gone right over the wall? said Shelley.

Don't be a twit, said Mick. There's a fucking great safety fence all around it.

Trying to breathe, Rachel lifted her head.

Where is he? she said.

What? said Dan. Where's who?

She looked at him, trying to think.

The man —

Shelley gave her a look.

You don't mean the guy in the Stetson? He was watching us all just now. A real creep. I don't like the look of him one bit.

Rachel blinked, shook her head.

Not him. Another man. He's staying at the resort.

What? Dan said again. Who is?

He came and talked to me. Just before I —

She broke off then, remembering the pale face, the keen chill of the hand, the flash of teeth. She shivered.

Hamilton, she said. He's called Hamilton.

Hamilton? Shelley repeated and everyone stared at her.

Dan hugged Rachel to him and kissed the side of her face.

I don't know about any man, sweetheart. We didn't
see a man. I think what we need to do right now is get
you some food.

Rachel looked at the scrubby ground where half a
discarded hot-dog bun lay, rimmed with ketchup.
Teeth marks in it.

I couldn't eat, she said.

Dan squeezed her shoulder till it hurt.

We'll see about that.

She stared at him.

And after all that, you only bloody well missed the
sun, said Mick.

It was ever so quick, Shelley said. And we didn't see
the green flash. But it was pretty cool, wasn't it, guys?

They sat at a long wooden table – jostled by other
people all laughing and talking and eating and
drinking – and watched the sky turn from puce, to
violet, to black. The harbour down below came alive
with lights. Mick and Shelley went and got plates of
fried chicken and beans and Dan said Rachel ought to
eat something too, but she reminded him about the
lobster dinner.

We're not going to eat till late, he said.

I'll be fine.

He held her eyes for a moment then he smiled.

OK. You're let off. Just this once.

He fetched her a bright orange drink and watched as she sniffed at it.

Orange juice, he said.

But what's in it?

He made an innocent face.

It's not just orange juice, she said. What's in it?

Shelley glanced at Dan.

The teeniest, tiniest shot of rum, she said. It's called a — I can't remember what it's called — Mick, what's it called?

Mick shrugged. His mouth was full of beans.

Drink it, darling, Dan said. I promise it will do you good.

Rachel had no intention of drinking it. What were they trying to do to her? But she kept one hand around the drink and the other on the place where the baby was growing safely inside her and, when enough time had passed, she got up and told them she was going to the loo.

You want me to come with you? Shelley offered, though she didn't put down her fork.

Rachel shook her head.

Don't be too long, Dan said, or we'll send a search party.

He was waiting for her right by the entrance to the Ladies. A tall, thin, shadowy form barely visible against the grey of the concrete. Even though she fully expected it, she still gasped as he put a cold hand on her wrist. His fingers tightening around her.

Just a few minutes, he said. I've been waiting.

What? she whispered. Why?

You know why.

Rachel said nothing. Heart banging, she glanced back at the others. She knew Dan would be straight over if he saw her talking to anyone. But she saw that he was laughing at something that Shelley had said, and when she managed to catch his eye, he just shrugged and blew her a kiss before turning back to his drink.

She didn't know how long they were together. It felt like ten minutes but it could have been an hour. She expected Dan to ask her why on earth she'd been so long, but instead he just smiled and patted the place he'd saved for her on the bench and helped her clamber back on. She felt his arm snake around her backside.

You didn't see him? she whispered.

What? he said. See who?

The man I was talking to.

Dan gazed at her.

Sorry? Talking to when?

She picked up the orange drink, but remembered in time and put it down again. She hesitated, trying to smooth out the strangeness of her voice – unable for a moment to remember how she normally spoke.

Just now. By the loos. He's staying at our resort. He's been there all this time. He was on the same flight as us, from London.

Dan didn't look very interested.

Well, so were a lot of other people, I imagine.

Yes, she said, faltering. He lost his luggage. Well, the airline did. All his holiday clothes. That's why he only has winter things with him. That's why he was wearing a suit on the beach.

She shut her eyes.

A grey suit. It's a grey woollen suit. Bespoke. He had it made many years ago. In London.

For a moment or two, they all stared at her. Shelley began to laugh.

How the hell do you know all that? Dan said.

Rachel blinked.

I don't know.

You don't know?

I don't know how I know it, no.

There was another bit of silence while everyone carried on looking at her. Then Mick burped.

Pardon me, he said.

Nice, said Shelley.

She bit into a drumstick.

Why doesn't he buy something from the shop then? she said. While he's waiting for them to find his luggage, I mean.

What do you mean? Rachel said.

Shelley shrugged.

Some trunks anyway. And shorts and a T-shirt. Whatever he needs. You don't walk around on the beach in a suit.

Not even a bespoke one, said Dan, laughing.

Shelley nodded.

He must be boiling. It's stupid. And he's wasting his holiday, isn't he?

Poor fucker, Mick said. And I bet the airline are denying all responsibility, too.

It's their fault, Shelley agreed. So they should buy him some stuff. I bet he's entitled to compensation for that. How long is he here for?

Rachel's heart was thumping. So many questions. They were making her dizzy.

Shelley licked her fingers.

How long? A week? Two weeks?

Rachel swallowed.

I don't know, she said. I really don't.

Shelley slumped on the bench and stared at her.

He doesn't mind not having trunks, Rachel said. He likes wearing his suit. And he's not a great swimmer anyway. He never learned to swim. Not properly.

That's unusual, Mick said. These days.

Dan was looking at her in a startled way.

You do seem to know an awful lot about this man, darling. It is pretty bloody strange. You seem to have his whole life story. I mean you can't have spoken to him for more than three minutes? Tonight's the first time you've met him, right?

Rachel looked down at the table.

I suppose so, she said.

You don't seem too sure, Mick said.

Shelley laughed.

Seriously, she said. How do you know all this?

I don't know, Rachel said. It's just – it's in my head, OK?

Shelley's eyes were still on her.

Now you're teasing, she said.

Dan took Rachel's hand, laced her fingers with his.

She's not teasing. You don't know Rachel. This is

83

what she's like. She isn't the type to tease. But she does have the imagination that bloody well ate Paris.

Seriously, though, he asked her later as they sat having the much-promised dinner in the little restaurant up on the hill. How did you know all that stuff?

Rachel looked at him. She suddenly knew that she didn't want to talk about any of it, ever, not ever again. She kept her face steady.

I told you, she said. He came and talked to me.

What, for a full three minutes and you found out all of that?

She shut her eyes for a second. Took a small breath.

I don't know. It's not important.

What did you say his name was again?

I can't remember, she lied.

Hamilton, was it?

I don't know, she said again, tearing off a bit of bread roll.

Dan was shaking his head.

Why does that name ring a bell?

She shrugged.

Oh dear. She frowned at the menu. I just don't know what to order.

This seemed to do the trick.

He smiled at her.

For god's sake, he said. You're having the lobster. It's what I brought you here for.

But do you think it's all right for the baby?

He was staring at the wine list.

If our child doesn't like lobster, then I'm dis-inheriting it right now.

Before she could say anything, he planted a kiss on her bare shoulder.

Joke. I'm sure it's OK. Honestly, Rach, stop fretting about everything all the time.

They shared a bowl of chilled soup (was it pea or was it avocado? – they couldn't decide) and talked about Dan's work – his column and his travel stuff and whether, with the baby coming, he could afford to take time off to write his book. They talked about the TV programme he sometimes went on and how his agent had told him it might be axed.

I don't care that much, he said. It's a hassle. It cuts into my week.

Rachel knew it wasn't true. She knew he loved going on TV. Even Rufus had been impressed when Dan had gone on TV.

Then they talked about Mick and Shelley. About

Shelley's terrible dress sense. About how come Mick had such a successful brother when he himself was such a layabout.

You don't know for sure that he's a layabout, Rachel said.

Dan smeared butter on his bread and threw it in his mouth.

He's had one job in the past five years. One job! He told me that with some pride.

He watched her as he chewed.

OK, Rachel said. He's a layabout.

They talked about Karen Keable's husband and how they hadn't laid eyes on him once since that first afternoon.

I reckon she's eaten him, Dan said.

Rachel laughed.

Think about it. He's so skinny and she's so big. It would explain a lot. Or maybe she's poisoned him and shoved him in a suitcase in their room.

Dan had ordered a bottle of champagne and insisted she had a glass, Rachel could feel it going straight to her head. She put the glass down.

Why would she come all the way to Antigua if she wanted to kill him? Why not just do it back in — wherever it is they live.

Bexleyheath, Dan said. They live in Bexleyheath.

And don't you know it's much, much easier to get away with murder if you're away? Home is home. Everyone knows where you are all the time. But if you're away, well, people have accidents, don't they?

Rachel shivered.

You seem to have given it some thought, she said.

He stroked a finger along the inside of her wrist.

Quite. So you'd better watch out. I still think she's eaten him, though.

The lobster was done in lime butter. It was the first thing in a long time she'd enjoyed eating.

You mean been willing to eat, Dan said.

She didn't bother correcting him. Instead, she concentrated on scraping it clean – extracting every single piece of flesh from every nook and cranny, every curve and crack and claw.

She was using the special steel tool to find any extra tufts of meat that she might have missed, and Dan was laughing and asking her if she'd like him to ask the waiter to have it put through a wringer, when she felt something and looked up.

The air fizzing and contracting. Her heart begin - ning to race.

You OK, darling? – Dan put a hand on her wrist – What's the matter? You look awful. You're white as a sheet.

Before she could think how to answer him, before she could even think, she got herself up from her seat. Trying to balance. She felt her napkin disengage itself from her knees and slip to the floor.

Air, she said.

What?

I need to get some air.

Dan was staring at her.

You feel faint?

No. Not faint. I just – I need to stand outside.

She heard his fork hit the plate. His chair pushed back.

I'm coming with you –

He began to get to his feet but she put a hand on his shoulder.

No, get off, leave me!

The words startled her. Coming out in too much of a shout. The waiter was coming over.

Now look what you've done, she said to Dan, her voice much harsher than she intended.

The waiter wanted to know if everything was OK.

It's fine, Dan said. We're fine. My wife just wants to get some air.

The waiter poured some water. Dan watched as she pretended to drink it. But he said nothing else. He stayed in his seat and watched as she moved away.

She felt wonderful as she moved, not faint at all. Alert and happy, the best she'd ever felt. She and the baby, in a perfectly protected bubble – floating, flying, immune and untouchable.

Better? Dan said when she came back and replaced herself in the seat opposite him.

She smiled, picked up her napkin. Saw the faint mouth-shape of her lipstick on it.

There's no need to interrogate me, she said.

His eyes crinkled with surprise.

I'm not interrogating. I'm concerned. I'm serious, Rach. Are you OK?

She nodded. Looked down at her plate. The lobster seemed a little worrying now. A smashed-up shell. The poor creature inside hadn't stood a chance. She looked quickly away.

I bumped into him again when I was outside, she said. Did you realise he was at school with you?

For a moment Dan's face was blank. His features were not his. Then they turned back into Dan again.

What? he said.

At school. Hamilton. He was in the year below you.

Dan's face tightened.

You saw him out there just now and he told you that?

Rachel picked up a lobster claw. Held it for a moment between her fingers. Its dark, brittle hardness. She didn't look at him but she nodded.

Mmm. Funny, isn't it?

She knew Dan was staring at her.

You were even in the same house, apparently.

She watched as Dan's jaw contracted.

Waverley? He was in Waverley?

That's right. He said he remembered Rufus too.

What? Dan said again, his amazement beginning to sound stupid now.

Rachel put down the claw. Wiped her fingers.

Well, he remembered that you two were friends.

Dan tilted his chair back and put his napkin on the table. He seemed to be thinking. At last, he shook his head.

No, he said. It's not possible. You're teasing me.

She looked up at him, her cheeks suddenly hot.

Of course I'm not teasing.

But – he can't have told you all of this. You mean outside just now?

Rachel tried to breathe.

He said you probably wouldn't remember him. He said he wouldn't be at all surprised if you denied it. He said it was a long time ago.

She heard Dan's quick, sharp breath.

Denied it? Denied what exactly?

She looked down at the table.

He said he didn't think he was very memorable. But he remembers you. You and Rufus. He remembers you very well.

Dan was silent for a moment.

And — ? he said at last.

What do you mean 'and'?

What else did he say?

Rachel folded her greasy napkin and pushed it away from her.

Nothing else. Why? Were you expecting something else?

The waiter brought the dessert menus. Rachel waved hers away, but Dan took his without looking and laid it on the table. She saw to her surprise that he was sweating. She watched as he wiped his face with a napkin.

I tell you, that really fucking creeps me out — he picked up the menu, looked at it, put it down again — What's his first name?

Rachel breathed very carefully.

I don't know it.

He hasn't told you?

I don't know. But do you remember him?

Dan's eyes widened.

What do you mean? Of course I bloody don't.

But you said just now that the surname rang a bell. Hamilton.

He hesitated.

What does he look like?

Rachel felt herself shiver.

Thin. Skinny. Dark-haired. Early twenties? she said before she could stop herself.

Dan laughed.

Early twenties? Well then. Come on, Rach. We can't have been at school together, can we?

Rachel struggled to think. Dan was thirty-six.

Or maybe older, she said. He's one of those people who could be any age.

Dan picked up the menu again. Confident now.

He's mistaking me for someone else, he said. And when has he seen me anyway? How does he even know what the hell I look like?

I don't know, Rachel told him truthfully.

He's made a mistake, Dan said again.

The waiter came and he ordered a sorbet and a coffee.

Two spoons? the waiter said.

No, said Rachel.

Yes, Dan said.

She looked at him.

Have you heard anything from Natasha yet? she asked him.

He thought for a second. He was fishing in his pockets for his cigarettes.

Natasha? Nothing at all, he said. Why?

I don't know. I was just thinking about her.

The sorbet came. With two spoons. Dan put his cigarettes on the table.

Me too, he said. I know. Poor Tash. Poor girl. I think about her all the fucking time.

In the night, Rachel woke and found herself alone in the bed. For a quick moment, she thought she was back at home in London, and that Dan was out at one of his parties or at the pub or —

Her heart was banging. She felt around for her bedside light, but it wasn't where it should be. And the bed was too high. And the bathroom door wasn't in the right place either.

And then she remembered. And saw that the door on to the terrace was open and he was out there.

Sitting on the edge of a chair in a T-shirt and boxers, elbows on his knees, smoking.

She sat up in the bed – still razzed from whatever it was that had woken her – and watched him for a moment, motionless, cigarette smoke drifting up through his fingers.

She slid out of bed and went to the bathroom and sat there in a kind of confusion, her face in her hands, her heart still thumping –

She saw that her feet were black – caked with dirt and earth, as if she'd been walking through the gardens with no shoes on. She stared at them for a moment. Then she ran water into the bidet – it wouldn't come warm so she made do with cold – and she washed both feet as quickly as she could with the tiny cake of soap and then dried them with the hand towel.

When she came back to bed, he was still out there. He hadn't moved at all. She thought about going out to him. But something stopped her. Instead she fell back to sleep and, because she hadn't been awake for long enough to shake herself out of it, straight back to where she'd just been.

Chapter Three

Dirt. On her face and in her mouth now. She sat up, gasping. It was morning and the room was beginning to be light. He was looking at her. Sitting there in his shorts and T-shirt. On the edge of the bed with a lighter in his hands.

She stared at him. There was something about the way he was sitting there that she didn't like. Her mouth was dry and her head hurt.

What time is it?

Are you all right? he said. You look – I don't know –

She didn't reply. With his eyes still on her, he pocketed the lighter.

I don't know what time it is. Early. I couldn't sleep, so I got up. Went for a walk. I didn't want to wake you.

She struggled to sit up.

What were you doing? she said.

He smiled.

You looked so gorgeous. Just lying there.

She gazed at him.

Don't, she said.

What?

Don't do that. Don't watch me. I don't like it.

He didn't look at her. He yawned and started to pull off his T-shirt.

She knew what he wanted. He wanted her to close her eyes and reach out for him, to take him in her arms, soft and trusting and sleepy and warm.

He slid a hand along her thigh.

Rachel? he whispered.

No, she said.

The taste of the dream was still on her. She swallowed it back. Earth and dirt. The memory of it, in her mouth. She remembered her filthy feet and turned away. She couldn't even look at him.

A few hours later, they walked up the path and through the main building to breakfast – and ran straight into a crowd of people and the flashing light of a police van.

They stopped. Dan put a hand on her arm.

My god, he said. What's happened?

Karen Keable was picking her way over the pebble path towards them. She looked older. Or maybe it was just that she didn't have her glasses on.

Isn't it awful? Unspeakable. In all the years Malcolm and I have been coming here – I just can't get my head around it.

Rachel felt her blood begin to jump.

What? What's happened? Has there been an accident?

Karen Keable's face wobbled. She had a balled-up tissue in her hand. She held it to her mouth and closed her eyes. Mick was standing with Shelley and a crowd of other guests. Dan went to speak to him. When he came back over, he took Rachel's hand in both of his.

A girl was found early this morning. On one of the paths down to the villas.

Rachel stared at him.

Found? What do you mean found?

One of the waitresses. Mick thinks they're saying she'd been strangled.

Rachel took a couple of steps backwards. The light was suddenly greasy, the sunshine no longer warm. She felt as if her legs might give way.

Come on, Dan said. We need to get you sitting down.

Several policemen in buff-coloured short-sleeved shirts were talking on radios. In their midst, walking up and down, Cedric in his white suit.

I'm all right, she said.

You're not all right.

Dan made her sit on the low stone wall. He fished around for a cigarette. Lit it. She watched his face as he inhaled, frowning. Karen Keable was looking at him.

They say there was screaming. Terrible screaming. In the night. Several people reported it. Someone even tried to call the concierge, but there was no one on duty. Don't you think that's shocking? You'd think there'd be someone on duty.

Rachel hugged herself. Her teeth were chattering. She looked at Karen Keable.

Who was it?

Karen Keable blinked at her.

Who was it? The waitress. What was her name?

Oh, I don't think anyone knows the girl's name. I do think there should have been someone on duty though. It's left me very unnerved indeed. The real question of course is how is this going to affect all of us? Every - where's taped off. You can't even get up to the spa. And people are being sent to the other beach apparently, which means there's going to be an almighty scramble

for umbrellas and towels, and if they can't accom-
modate everyone, well, all hell will break loose, won't it?

Rachel wanted to skip breakfast, but he wouldn't let
her.

I don't care what's happened, he said. I don't care if
the entire resort's exploded and gone into orbit. We're
here now. You're eating something.

They were there, but no one else was. The room was
silent, almost empty. Only the sparrows enjoying an
uninterrupted feast. A handwritten cardboard sign
apologised for the lack of any hot food. They saw the
woman who usually cooked the omelettes being
ushered out, in tears.

He went and got a croissant and pulled it apart and
fed it to her. At first she resisted but then she let him.
Encouraged, he tried to put butter on it, but she
refused that. Pastry flakes falling down the front of
her T-shirt. Swallowing back tears.

This is ridiculous, she said. I'm not an invalid.

He touched the milk jug to see if it was hot. Poured
milk into his coffee. Put a cup of tea into her hands
and waited while she drank.

I don't trust you. I know you. You won't eat a thing
unless I force you.

He laid a hand on her bare leg.

Look, he said. This is still our honeymoon.

She said nothing.

It's our special time, Rach. It's not going to come again.

She gazed at him.

What's that supposed to mean?

It means we can't let this get in the way of anything.

She pushed his hand off her leg and moved her chair back.

A young girl is dead, she said.

He swallowed coffee, pressed the napkin to his lips. Then he picked up another piece of croissant, began to butter it.

They went back to their room to get their things and decide what to do. Outside, the sun was already hot, the sky cloudless.

He put his arm around her as they walked down the clean white steps and past the pool, its turquoise water wobbling in the bright sunlight.

I wasn't going to tell you this, but I had an email from Natasha –

She twisted free to look at him.

Had an email when?

Last night. Well, very early this morning. I didn't want to wake you. But listen, it's the strangest thing. They're saying that Rufus was caught on a speed camera –

She made a noise of surprise.

Rufus? Speeding?

He looked at her.

Of course not. Good old safety-conscious Rufus? He wouldn't have been caught dead speeding –

He hesitated, hearing himself.

But Tash says that if an accident is unexplained, they look at the camera footage. And – this is the part I just can't get my head around – it seems there was someone else in the car with him.

Rachel stopped walking.

Someone else? How could there possibly have been someone else?

Dan ran his hands through his hair.

I know, I know. But the footage clearly shows another person. According to the police, anyway.

Rachel stared at him.

Male or female?

What?

A man or a woman?

Dan blinked.

I don't know. I don't know how clear the footage is.

But — when they found him? Was there someone else?

Of course not. Just Rufus in the car. We know that. Without any doubt.

Rachel took a breath.

Well, then. It's not possible, is it?

What's not possible?

They must be wrong.

Dan shrugged.

Except that cameras don't lie.

Maybe it was faulty? Maybe they've got it mixed up and it was footage of another car?

Dan was silent a moment.

They've got the whole accident on tape, Rach. That day, that time, Rufus's car. Tash is pretty upset, obviously.

Neither of them said anything. They walked on till they reached the door of their room.

Why weren't you going to tell me? she said as he got the key out.

What?

You said you weren't going to tell me. Why not?

He looked at the ground for a moment.

It's like I just said. This is our honeymoon. It won't come again. And what can we possibly do about it anyway?

*

She went straight into the bathroom and locked the door, stood there for a moment, shut her eyes, tried to take some breaths. Then she flushed the toilet and went back into the bedroom.

Dan was lying on the unmade bed flicking through the channels. He found local TV. Photos of the hotel came up. The resort taken from above – beaches, pools, the startling green of the golf course, the glittering sea.

The police commissioner was called Gary Lomax. He was asking guests to come forward. Anyone who might have heard or seen anything, however small or insignificant it might seem, in the night. He said that cause of death was still unknown. For a few seconds, a shot of a girl came on the screen. She was wearing school uniform, her hair up in a topknot. It was Hortensia and she looked as if someone had just told her a joke. The screen switched to a view of the hotel grounds and, just visible among the trees, a white tent.

Dan flicked it off and stood up.

Come on. It's glorious out there. We're not going to stay holed up in our room watching murder TV.

Rachel looked down and saw that she had a bathroom towel in her hand. She didn't remember carrying it through. She flung it on the bed.

You should talk to them, she said.

What?

Like he said. They want people who might have seen or heard things.

Dan didn't look at her. He was fiddling with the screen door.

What do you mean? he said.

I saw you. In the middle of the night. Out there, on the terrace. You were there for ages. You should tell them. In case you heard something.

He stopped what he was doing and looked at her. His face stayed smooth and tight.

Sweetheart, he said. What on earth are you talking about? I didn't go anywhere. You were the one who got up.

What?

You don't remember? You went out there, on the terrace. You said you couldn't sleep. A bad dream or something.

Rachel felt her heart speed up.

I couldn't sleep?

I don't know exactly what you said. I tried to com - fort you but I was half asleep myself, to be honest.

She watched as he went out onto the terrace. She saw him pick up his trunks which had been drying on the back of a chair. He smacked them hard against the railing to get the sand off them. He came back in.

You honestly don't remember? he said.

She said nothing. She found her own swimming costume, stuffed it into her bag. Looked around for her sunglasses and sun cream. Her book, though she couldn't imagine wanting to read it.

It's not true, she said. I didn't get up.

He hesitated and she heard him sigh.

I did wake up early this morning, he said. But I was only awake because of Tash's email. I told you — it woke me up, got me thinking. I suppose it upset me a bit. I couldn't sleep at all after that. That's why I was sitting watching you sleep this morning.

He looked at her for a second. Then he rubbed at his chin, dipped his head to look in the mirror.

Should I shave, do you think? Or shall I not bother?

They ran into Karen Keable on their way down to the beach. She told them that some guests were thinking of shipping straight out, asking for their money back.

Some of the first-timers are extremely alarmed, she said. They all think they're going to get murdered in their beds now. I hear there's pressure on Cedric to bring in a security firm.

This got Dan's attention.

And do you think he will?

Karen Keable shrugged.

Not that it would make a blind bit of difference. The security people are all thick with the criminals. And the police aren't much better. A bunch of thugs, the lot of them. When Malcolm and I first started coming here, this really did feel like a safe place. Go to Antigua, we used to tell our friends. It's the closest thing to paradise you'll find on this earth. I certainly wouldn't say that now.

She looked at Rachel.

And what about you, my dear? Are you feeling all right? This has rather taken the gloss off things, hasn't it? Do you think you'll stay?

Of course we're staying, Dan said. We wouldn't dream of leaving, would we, Rach?

Rachel hesitated. For a moment or two, the idea had made her heart lift. A speedily arranged flight. The homely grey of Gatwick Arrivals. Tigger yowling and wrapping himself around her ankles. Her own bed.

She looked at Dan. His hand already going to his pocket for a cigarette. She looked at Karen Keable and smiled.

I think we want to give it a bit longer, she said.

*

They went down onto the beach. For once they had their pick of umbrellas.

That was nice of you, he said. Considering we both know you'd do anything to get the hell out of here.

Rachel spread her towel over her lounger, got out the sunscreen, a bottle of water, her book.

We're here now, aren't we? she said.

Dan was dragging his lounger right around in the sand so it faced into the sun.

Anyway, the place is full of police. I doubt they're going to let people up sticks and leave the island just like that.

Rachel thought about the long paths down to the villas. The grass damp and green from the sprinklers. Dan was pulling off his shirt. Energetic, eager. She found herself staring at his stomach – the hard flatness of muscle, the little swirl of hairs below his navel –

He stopped.

What? What's the matter now?

She twisted her hair up into a knot. Squirted sun cream into the palm of her hand.

I don't know what you mean, she said.

Dan looked at the sea and then he looked back at her.

Go on, she said, because she could see that he was dying to go. Go for your swim. What are you waiting for?

He smiled. Then he picked her book up off the towel, opened it and handed it to her. He bent and kissed her.

When I come back I'll go to the bar. Get us something nice to drink.

She sat there for a moment, the book heavy in her hands. Then she shut it, frowning.

You want me to come in with you? she said.

He looked startled.

What?

In the water? Do you want me to come?

She saw him hesitate.

Well, you can. Of course you can. But, well, I thought I might just strike out properly – get a bit of a workout. You don't mind, do you, darling?

Rachel shook her head. She didn't mind. Or if she did, she couldn't think of a single reason why that might be.

She let her book drop down into the sand. Then she leaned back and shaded her eyes and watched him go.

As soon as Dan left, she felt it. This time she wasn't surprised. It was what she expected. That as soon as she was alone, he would find her.

It was the bright hot middle of the day, the sun

high in the sky, and this time she was alert, tensed, ready for it. She kept on looking around her, waiting, daring it, almost hoping –

She knew it was coming because she'd never been so cold. Shivering and glancing down at her two bare knees, her much too pale thighs, goosepimpling, the chipped polish on her toes, the child inside her, hanging there.

She suddenly wished she'd kept her sundress on.

And then –

A pair of hands grabbing onto her legs. Two pale, skinny, dirty hands, scratched and bleeding, the nails torn and ragged, cuticles rimmed with dirt –

Her breath came tearing from her chest in one long cry but before she could do any more, it had gone. The sun was hot. The air, the light, it changed. It was over. He was gone.

Next time she looked, there was Dan, coming up the beach, shaking the water from his hair.

Rain, he said.

What?

Look at the sky.

She looked. All the blue had gone and the sky was metallic and one or two raindrops were already darkening the sand.

*

A tropical storm. A squall. That's what they were saying in the little bar above the beach. People stood or sat around, drinking and smoking and playing dominoes and waiting for it to stop.

You think this is rain? – an elderly Australian stood watching the inky sky with a two-day-old copy of *The Times* on his head – You should come here in the hurricane season if you want to see a decent storm.

Yeah, well maybe that's why we didn't book for the bloody hurricane season, Mick said under his breath.

He and Shelley were perched on bar stools, towels draped around their shoulders, drinking pina coladas.

Rachel felt Shelley looking her up and down.

Did you get caught? she said. We did. Look at us. We got completely soaked.

You guys want anything? Dan said. I'm going to the bar.

We're good, thanks, Shelley said.

Rachel told him she didn't want anything. Shelley told her she should have something. Mick tried to offer her his stool but she told him she'd rather stand.

They all stared out at the sea. Rain tipped itself out of the sky in straight lines. Sour yellow flashes lit the horizon. A radio behind the bar was playing 'Boogie Nights'. A girl with a badge that said *Priscilla* was wiping the counter.

Must be some kind of a freak storm, Mick said, coming out of nowhere like this.

Shelley wiped her straw around the top of her glass.

Not out of nowhere, she said. The guy in the lobby knew about it.

Mick looked at her.

What guy?

You know. The guy. The one who deals with all the luggage and stuff.

Well, there was nothing on the blackboard by the desk, Mick said.

Shelley bit her lip.

I guess they had more pressing things to do today than write up the weather forecast.

Everyone was silent for a moment. They watched as Dan came back, empty-handed.

That was quick, Mick said.

Dan shrugged.

Couldn't be bothered to queue. I'll go again in a minute.

Cedric's the one I feel sorry for, Mick said.

What? said Dan.

Can't be the greatest thing for business, something like this.

Dan nodded.

Wonder how long it will take them to catch him.

JULIE MYERSON

The guy in the Coralita bar told me they're saying she was definitely strangled, said Mick.

They used the belt off her uniform, Shelley said. Poor little lass.

It'll turn out to be someone who knew her, Dan said. Bet you anything. A relative or a boyfriend or something.

Rachel looked at him.

Why? she said.

He shrugged.

Because it always is, isn't it?

There was a pause.

Some of the guests are leaving, Shelley said. I wouldn't leave. Lose my whole holiday? No way. Would you leave?

Dan put his arm around Rachel and pulled her against him.

We're not going anywhere, are we, Rach?

Mick finished his drink and looked at Dan.

Still, I wouldn't mind getting away from the resort, though. Just for the day or something. We were thinking about taking one of those catamaran tours to Green Island. You guys ever think of doing that?

Shelley sighed.

I'm not sure I fancy it. Trapped on a boat all day with a bunch of strangers.

You could always charter one yourselves, Dan said.

Mick looked doubtful.

What, you mean privately? With someone to sail it for you?

You get a skipper. And they throw in lunch, drinks and whatever, Dan said.

Mick looked at him.

It's an idea. Bet it costs an arm and a leg, though?

Dan hesitated.

You're right, it's not cheap.

Any idea how much exactly?

Dan looked away. Rachel saw that he was blushing. Dan never blushed. He stared at the ground.

Depends on how many people, of course. But I think you're talking in the region of six or seven hundred dollars for two of you —

Mick whistled. Rachel looked at Dan.

How do you know?

What do you mean how do I know?

About what they cost?

He shrugged.

I don't know how I know. It's in that folder of stuff in our room, isn't it?

Mick wiped his mouth.

Well, thanks anyway, mate, that sounds promising. I might look into it.

JULIE MYERSON

Better than going with a whole load of fat tourists, Shelley said. She looked at Rachel. Hey, you sure you don't want me to budge up so you can sit down?

Dan said he was going to have another try at getting a beer. Mick and Shelley still didn't want anything. Rachel asked for a glass of water, no ice. Dan rolled his eyes at Mick and Shelley.

She thinks it contains bacteria.

Well, Shelley said. You can't be too careful when you're pregnant.

When he'd gone, she turned to Rachel.

So when are you due?

Rachel told her July.

And I hear you've been having quite a rough time of it?

Rachel looked down at where the baby was. She smoothed her hands over her dress.

Not really, she said, seeing Shelley glance at Mick. Why? What's he been telling you?

Mick smiled and Shelley laughed.

Don't worry, she said. It's all good.

We kind of bonded with Dan on the first night, Mick said. Partly through knowing Natasha and all that –

114

It was just so awful, Shelley said. About Rufus. And for you especially the timing must have been terrible. Such a shock. You must have been so shaken up.

He pretty much told us your entire life story, Mick said.

I think he's just concerned about you, Shelley added.

He's a good bloke, said Mick.

For a moment, Rachel felt confused.

Rufus was much more his friend than mine, she said.

That's right, Shelley said. Schooldays. He said. All the same, though – and Natasha's such a lovely person.

There was a pause. The rain was easing off. Rachel flicked a glance at the bar. She saw that Dan was hunched over a piece of paper, writing something. She watched as he handed it to the barman.

She threw Shelley what she hoped was a convincing smile.

She is, she said. She's lovely.

The rain had almost stopped, but the sky stayed sullen and grey. People were moving away from the bar. Shelley asked Rachel if she'd guard her bag while she went to the toilet. Dan finished his beer and got up and stood leaning against the wooden rail, smoking a cigarette.

It looks like it's going to brighten up, he said. I give it half an hour. How about we grab a fresh fish sandwich at that little place we saw near the scuba hut?

Rachel glanced back at Mick who was putting coins in the cigarette machine.

You mean just us?

Of course just us. Who else?

She shivered and fished around in her bag for her cardigan.

I don't know why you keep on being so friendly to those two.

He glanced at her in surprise.

I thought you were being friendly too. I thought you liked them. Anyway I want to stay in touch with Mick — because of his brother, remember?

Rachel said nothing. Shelley came back. She delved in her bag and pulled out a mirror and lip gloss.

What are you guys doing now anyway? she said.

Dan slid an arm around Rachel's waist.

I'm spiriting my wife away for a romantic lunch à deux. If I don't, I think divorce might be on the cards.

Shelley, putting gloss on, smiled a tight little smile.

You're on your honeymoon, aren't you? You should do exactly what you want.

She checked her lips, then snapped the mirror shut and picked up her bag. She smiled at Dan.

If you need to blow off some steam, you know where we are.

As she clattered off down the steps in her wooden mules, Rachel looked at him.

What did she mean by that?

What?

Blow off steam? Why would you need to blow off steam?

Dan kissed the side of her neck.

I've absolutely no idea. She's a funny girl, isn't she, but she's OK. A bit loud, but I think she means well.

By the time they got to the Sugar Bay Grill, the clouds had parted and the sea was bright. A fat rainbow spilled its colours into the bay, but the beach stayed empty. The sand was damp. The cabin where they gave out the cushions and towels was padlocked.

Dan asked the man who was cooking the fish when it would open again. He shrugged.

More rain is coming.

Dan looked up at the sky.

Really? Are you sure?

The man grinned and showed a mouthful of gold teeth.

The Caribbean is full of surprises.

Dan laughed.

I'll say.

He leaned over and squeezed Rachel's knee.

Ouch, she said. That hurt.

They ordered two fish rolls with chilli sauce and mayonnaise and a tomato and cucumber side salad.

I don't even care if it is wahoo, Dan said as he pulled open his roll and peered inside. I've been wanting one of these ever since I walked past and smelled them cooking yesterday.

He took a bite and looked at Rachel.

Come on, he said, his mouth full. Isn't a man even allowed to enjoy his lunch now? Seriously, Rach, you've got to cheer up or I may have to go and get myself a new wife.

Rachel looked down at her plate.

What were you writing? she asked him.

What?

Back there in the bar. I saw you write something and give it to the barman.

For a moment, Dan looked startled. Then he relaxed.

Oh, it's just that there's something wrong with our safe. I was seeing if he could ask Cedric to send someone along to fix it.

Rachel frowned.

You mean the safe in our room?

That's the one.

You never told me that there was something wrong with it. You didn't say anything.

Dan smeared mayonnaise along the edge of his roll.

Well, I didn't know, did I? Until I went to get my wallet out this morning and it wouldn't close properly. It's hardly the end of the world, but I'm not all that keen on having it sitting there half open with cleaners and whoever else coming and going.

He put down the knife. Rachel watched as he took another bite of the roll.

But why didn't you tell me that it was broken?

This morning, you mean? With all due respect, my darling, I think your mind was on other things.

Rachel thought about this.

But when did you see that it was broken? Before we left our room? Because we didn't find out about — what had happened — until after we left our room.

Dan's face hardened. He swallowed and put his roll down on the plate.

Christ. What is this? I didn't realise I was in for a

full-scale police interrogation. What's the matter? What exactly are you accusing me of?

She gazed at him for a moment. She picked up her glass and took a sip of water.

I'm sorry, she said.

She put the glass back down, looked at it. Dan folded a slice of cucumber and wiped it through the mayonnaise left on his plate.

Oh god, he said as he put it in his mouth. It's the great big conspiracy thing again, isn't it?

She raised her head.

What do you mean?

All of it. Everything. This place. The voodoo stuff. The scary warnings that I'm about to die. The furniture that jumps around of its own accord. And now, oh my god, the safe.

He hesitated, licking his fingers. They were both silent for a moment. At last, he reached out, put a hand on her thigh.

Look, are you going to eat something? Or do I have to force-feed you as usual?

Rachel bit into her roll. Chewed and swallowed. It tasted of nothing.

What happened at school? she said. With Rufus. When you were kids. Teenagers. Did something bad happen?

Dan's mouth fell open.

What on earth – where the fuck did that question come from?

Rachel didn't know where it had come from. She swallowed.

Did you – did you ever do anything to anyone?

Anything? What do you mean by anything?

Rachel said nothing.

Dan waited and then he put down his roll and wiped his fingers. He seemed to take a long time doing it. When he finally looked at her, his eyes were cold.

I don't understand. What exactly are you asking me?

Rachel pulled a bit of bread off her sandwich, but she didn't eat it. She looked up and saw the light on the sea – glittering like a toothache.

I don't know, she said at last.

He made a noise of impatience. He pushed his plate away. Then he seemed to have second thoughts and pulled it back. He stared at it. He swallowed. When he spoke, his voice was rough with emotion.

Is this what you want? he said. You want to do this now? On our honeymoon?

Rachel was surprised to feel herself go quite still inside. He was staring at her. She dared herself to meet his gaze.

Do what? she said.

*

But later as the clouds came rolling across the sky, and they gave up on the beach and strolled the long way back to their room, he turned to her.

It was him, wasn't it?

What?

That creep. Suit guy. The one who said he remembered me from school. He's stirred you up somehow. I can tell. You've been thinking about what he said.

It had begun to rain again. They moved under an awning and leaned against the smooth white wall, watching the pool, listening to the sound of rain hitting the palms. One lone swimmer swam up and down the pool. Beyond him, in the shelter of the bar, kids played ping-pong, laughing. The ball clattered as it bounced.

Dan held his cigarette out to the side, away from her. He watched the smoke.

I could tell you everything if you wanted me to, he said. Every miserable detail of my fucking miserable childhood.

She stayed silent for a moment, watching the swimmer.

Was it a miserable childhood?

Dan sucked on the cigarette. He didn't look at her.

You know it was. I've told you.

Rachel frowned, trying to remember what he'd told her. She knew that his father had died young and his mother had a problem with alcohol. But Dan had always been vague about his family. He didn't like to talk about the past. Whenever she pressed him, he became silent and withdrawn, angry even. She'd soon learned not to do it.

You mean at school?

He flicked ash off his cigarette. Keeping his head turned away from her. She heard him take a breath.

I know you love to say money isn't important, Rach. But you've always had it. In the background. Somewhere. Wherever. It's always been there for you. A big, fat, comfortable cushion to lean back on if you need to. So you can't begin to understand what it feels like to be thirteen and hard up. And to be sent off to a place where you stick out like a sore thumb because you're the only one —

But, Rachel said, how come your mother could afford to send you to — ?

Dan laughed.

My mum had nothing to do with it. Well, except as a recipient of her brother's charity. She drank my father's money away. But I suppose my uncle thought he was being kind. He had no kids and he was loaded. He chose the school and paid the

fees. A good education, make a man of me and all
that —

He sighed and looked at Rachel.

But you know, in a way I think I'd have been
much better left exactly where I was. With my own
kind. So, to answer your question, yes, lots of bad
things happened at school. To me and to other people.
I suppose the truth is I've tried to forget them.

The rain was falling hard now. The air had turned
grey. The swimmer had got out. People were shrieking
and running for cover.

They stayed under the awning. Dan pulled up a
chair for her and she sat down, watching the rain pour
down. She put her hands back on the faint, hardening
curve of the baby and waited —

At last he threw his cigarette on the ground.

I don't want to hide anything from you, Rachel, he
said. You know that.

She didn't reply. Did she know it? She wasn't sure if
she did. He tried to take her hand, but she wouldn't let
him. Instead she kept her fingers pressed tight over her
belly. And then at last, there it was. The faintest little
flutter —

He touched her hand.

Forgive me? he said.

She shook her head.

Don't be silly. There's nothing to forgive.

The baby shifted under her hands.

Is it moving? he said. Can you feel it?

She bit her lip. The movement was intense. Her womb had never felt more chaotic and alive.

She looked up at him.

No, she said. Not right now. I don't think so.

Back in their room, she lay down on the bed and watched as he went over and drew the blind. A black shadow fell across the room. Then he pulled off all his clothes and went into the bathroom, not quite closing the door.

As soon as she heard him lift the seat, she slipped out of bed and hurried over to the cupboard. She pulled it open and tried the grey metal door of the safe. It wouldn't move. It was locked. She tried it again. Definitely locked. As it should be. As she'd thought it was.

She slid back into bed and turned on the TV. It was Michael Caine in *The Italian Job* with French subtitles. But before she could zap through the channels to find the local news, Dan had leapt across and snatched the remote from her hand.

Nice try, he said.

He aimed it at the set and turned it off.

I just wanted to see if they'd arrested anyone, she said.

We'll find out soon enough.

He turned and threaded his arms around her, under her. Kissed her nose. Slid a hand between her legs. She tensed.

Come on, he said.

You act as if this whole thing hasn't happened, she said.

What?

The poor girl. Don't you even want them to find out who did it?

He kissed her shoulder.

It's not my problem, is it?

Dan, she said. For god's sake —

You're worried there's a murderer on the loose? I'll protect you.

He laughed and pulled her on top of him and he kissed her and she tried to kiss him back, but she couldn't. She didn't want to. Her body felt hard and worried and upset. She rolled off.

He was silent for a moment.

What is it? he said at last. Why can't you relax?

She tried to steady herself.

Isn't it obvious?

He came closer. He touched her head. Then he

took a strand of her hair and played with it, twisting it round his finger. He tried to look into her eyes but she wouldn't let him.

No, he said. It isn't obvious.

She felt him looking at her.

All right, he said. You don't want to be here, do you? You want to go home.

She shut her eyes for a second.

It's not that.

What is it, then?

She said nothing. They lay there in silence.

What is it? he said again.

She shivered and he pulled her to him.

Come here, he said. You're cold.

I'm not.

You are, he said as he held her tighter. Your arms. I can feel it. You're freezing. You feel like a zombie. One of the undead.

It was supposed to make her laugh, but it did the opposite. It made her grow dark and sad. They lay there together and she watched the fan go round and round and waited for her blood and her heart to calm down. She could hear from his breathing that he was almost asleep. She remembered what she wanted to ask him.

Did they mend it yet?

What?

She felt him jerk awake.

The safe. Did Cedric get the message? Did he send someone to come and do it?

He took her hand and held it for a moment. Then he yawned and let go of it again.

I don't think so, he said.

She felt herself stiffen.

So it's still broken? It still won't close?

He reached out and patted her thigh.

Shh, he said. Not now.

She slept for five minutes or maybe it was half an hour – so many sensations and ideas collapsed within it – and woke to something calling her name. More a feeling than a sound. She sat up, every muscle and nerve in her body alert to it. Leaving Dan sleeping, she pulled on her dress and picked up her sandals and crept from the room.

It was late afternoon. The rain had stopped and the sun was bright, the air rinsed and sweet. She hurried down the steps and past the small pool. Two teenage girls in bikinis were hunched together, trailing their legs in the water and talking in low voices. They went quiet as she passed them, but as she moved away, they started up again.

Every time she stopped and listened, she could feel him.

She walked on up the shallow gravel path towards reception where the police vans were parked. A bunch of men in buff-coloured uniforms sat drinking cans of Pepsi. They looked tired and bored. One of them kept his eyes on her legs as she walked up the steps. She moved faster.

Inside, a skinny boy in a baseball cap was cleaning the floor, eyes closed, headphones vibrating with noise as he dragged the machine along. She skirted around him – tang of lemon and ammonia – and went into the shop.

The shop wasn't closed but it felt closed – the lights dim and the door propped open with a crate of Evian bottles. Behind the counter on a high stool, a woman was leafing through a magazine. She put it down when Rachel came in.

The smell was overpowering. Candles and soaps and things that didn't need to be scented, but were. Rachel pretended to inspect the racks of bikinis and kaftans and bottles of Antiguan rum and Susie's Hot Chilli Sauce. She picked up a marbled glass ashtray, turned it over to look at the price.

The woman's eyes followed her.

Anything I can help you with today?

Rachel told her she was just looking. She picked up a furiously red piece of soap.

Passion fruit, the woman said. Made right here on the island. But we have Dove and Nivea if you prefer.

Rachel took a large bottle of water from the fridge and put it on the counter, along with a bag of crisps. She didn't want the water or the crisps. She was just about to count out the money when she saw the biros on a rack by the till.

She picked one up. A tiny ship sliding downwards in a bubble of liquid.

The woman smiled as she rang it up.

Present for someone back home?

Rachel nodded. For an unlikely moment or two, she really did see herself safely back home, curled on the sofa in front of the TV, drinking tea.

The bar next to the shop was dark and deserted. Disco playing on a radio somewhere. On the terrace, a boy who looked no more than twelve or thirteen was sweeping the ground between the tables. She saw Cedric in his white suit coming along the path towards her and her heart sank.

Caribbean Calypso Evening, he said before she

could pretend she hadn't seen him. Seven o'clock. You have to try the Smile.

She must have looked confused, because he rubbed his hands together.

Our signature cocktail. The famous Antiguan Smile. Rum, banana and pineapple.

Rachel looked down at the bottle of water in her hands and shook her head.

Is there any news? she said.

Cedric's smile dropped away.

News?

Have they arrested anyone?

Cedric looked at her for a second, then the phone in his pocket buzzed. He took it out, held up a finger and shook his head.

I have to take this, he said.

He took a couple of steps away from her.

Waterside Bar, he called out as he waved and walked away. Here by the pool. Seven o'clock sharp. No excuses. Tell your husband Cedric said so.

She went back into reception. She already knew what the answer to her question would be, but she needed to hear someone say it. The woman's name badge said *Marlene – Here to Help*.

Rachel explained that she and her husband had promised one of the guests they'd try and hook up for a drink, only they didn't know his room number. The woman told her she couldn't give out a room number, but she could leave a message on the guest's phone.

You have the surname?

Yes, Rachel said. Hamilton.

Rachel watched as the woman went over to a computer. Bent down and keyed something in. Waited, frowning.

She looked up.

And the first name?

Rachel hesitated.

I don't have a first name.

The woman looked at her for a second.

Can you tell me the spelling? Of the surname?

Rachel told her.

She bit her lip and squinted at the screen again.

And you don't have a first name?

No, Rachel said.

Then are you sure of the surname? she said. Because we've not had anyone of that name staying here even in the past few years. Our computer records go back some way.

Rachel sighed. Then it struck her.

If I told you he was the guy whose luggage got lost?

You were trying to track it down for him. Does that help?

The woman threw her a blank look.

None of our guests have lost any luggage recently.

Rachel felt her heart speed up.

Maybe someone else was dealing with it?

I'm the service manager here, she said. I'd know about it. And like I say, no one's had any luggage go astray recently. Virgin have a pretty good track record actually.

As Rachel gave up and turned to walk away, the woman called her back. She was grinning.

Excuse me, but – you're meeting the guy for a drink and you're gonna call him by his surname?

Rachel flushed and then she shrugged.

I know. It's an old English public school thing. Ridiculous, isn't it?

She left reception and walked back out into the bright sunshine, past the sprinklers flicking water over the short grass, and up towards the swimming pool. Straight away, it was there – she felt it. Arms grabbing her, sharp and certain, not letting go. She smelled an animal scent, like old earth, felt the staleness of hair in her face. Black hair. His hair.

No! she said — and somewhere in her bones she felt the vibration as he told her yes.

He hugged her hard and everything stopped. The sprinklers, the birds, the heat of the sun. For a moment they were both in darkness and she was struggling to breathe. Then, just as quickly, they were somewhere else. Standing in front of the wide and blowy Atlantic ocean. The wind roaring in her ears —

She staggered backwards, looking around her. The beach was dirty. Rubbish littering the sand. Black seaweed strewn around. A broken umbrella, battered by the wind, its skeleton exposed. She smelled rotten eggs.

She tried to look at his face, but he would not let her. Instead, gripping her by the shoulders, he turned her around to face the cliffs, pushed her head back and jabbed a bloodless finger, pointing upwards.

You see up there?

He had her hair in his fist, tugging, tilting her head back hard so she had to look. High above them perched on the cliff was a villa with a wide terrace that looked right out over the ocean. She saw it all — the bright cobalt blue of a painted wooden veranda that went all the way around. Purple bougainvillea tumbling over it and down the low wall. Beneath, a sheer drop down on to the rocks.

She could hear his breath in her ear, the rasp of his voice.

That's it, he said. That's the place.

What? she gasped. What place?

It's where you'll go. Where you'll do it.

Do what?

It's what she would have asked if she could have. But as soon as she opened her mouth, there she was, beneath the ground. A dull darkness thudding down around her. Dirt on her face, in her eyes, up her nose and in her mouth. She did scream then – screamed and cried out and scrabbled hard with her fingers, feeling her nails jag and rip, the weight of earth on her shoulders, elbows, wrists –

And then –

And then everything stopped and it let go and was gone and it was just her standing alone on the bright green grass with the birds calling and the sprinklers still flicking their rainbow drops in the soft afternoon light.

When she got back, Dan was on the terrace, pacing up and down and smoking a roll-up. Damp from his shower. A towel wrapped around his waist. He looked upset.

Where the fuck have you been?

For a walk, she said.

Well, you might have left me a note or something. You've been gone for ever. I was worried.

She swallowed. She felt trembly and light. Thirsty. She opened the fridge, took out a bottle of water. She glanced in the mirror. Dirt on her face. Every bone in her body ached. Her hands were shaking. She couldn't get the bottle open. She put it down and held them out to him.

Look, she said. Look what happened.

His face was blank.

What?

My hands.

She held them right up to his face. He looked.

What about them?

She glanced down at her scratched and dirty hands. The fingernails were even worse than she'd thought — ripped and broken, the cuticles rimmed with blood. She took a breath, trying to steady herself.

For god's sake, Dan — look at them!

He gazed at her.

What? he said. What am I supposed to be looking at?

She took a breath. Looked down at them again. Her heart raced. She turned them over, searching for scratches — for anything at all. She began to cry.

Dan was looking at her.

Darling, he said.

He took hold of her hands, gently inspecting them – nails, backs, palms. Her tanned fingers, clean nails. The innocent gleam of her wedding ring. Concern was all over his face.

What's going on? Rachel, you've got to tell me.

She swallowed. Still trembling, she unscrewed the lid of the bottle.

I went down to the ocean, she said. On the other side.

She tipped her head back and drank. Cool liquid down the back of her throat. It felt good. He was standing watching her, his face upset and uncertain.

The other side?

The Atlantic side. It's windy there.

On your own?

She blinked. Remembering the roar of the ocean and the bright blue veranda. The terrace with the purple flowers tumbling down. The icy grip of his hands on her shoulders.

Of course on my own. Who would I go with? I'm not a child, she added.

She drank from the bottle again. Dan made a noise of impatience. He threw off his towel and started pulling on his boxers. He grabbed his shirt off the chair.

Last night someone was murdered, he said. Just last night. A matter of hours ago. And now you go wandering off on your own?

For a moment, she froze.

But there are police everywhere. You said it yourself.

He said nothing. He pulled on his shorts and went out onto the terrace to get his drink and his sunglasses. She heard him sigh. She sat down on the bed, kicked off her shoes.

She looked at her hands again. Her heart was thumping.

Who were you talking to just now? she said.

She heard him put down his drink.

He hesitated.

What do you mean? I wasn't talking to anyone.

Yes you were. Just now. Before I came back.

He was silent for a moment. Then he appeared in the doorway.

Before you came back? I was talking to Natasha. But that was ages before you came back. At least ten or fifteen minutes.

Oh, she said.

He came over to her.

You weren't here. So how could you possibly know that?

She thought for a second.

I don't know, she said.

For a moment, his eyes narrowed.

You weren't listening, were you?

What? – she glanced up in surprise – Why on earth would I do that?

No, he said. Sorry. Of course you wouldn't.

He stood there for another moment, looking lost. Then he widened his eyes.

Do you mind? he said.

Mind what?

That I was talking to her?

She shrugged. She didn't know if she minded or not. She minded the fact that he maybe wouldn't have told her. Little lies that weren't really lies, piling up all the same.

And what about the safe? she said. Did they fix it?

He sat down on a chair. He looked fed up.

No, they bloody didn't. And I don't expect them to get around to it any time soon. I'm a bit pissed off about it actually. I don't know what I'm supposed to do about our stuff.

Rachel got up and marched over to the cupboard where the safe was. Pulled it open. The door of the safe also swung open.

He was watching her.

You see? The red light's on. As if it's locked. But it's

not locked. And even when I key in the numbers, the green light doesn't come on.

She stared at it – tried to shut it. It wouldn't shut. Something was definitely jamming it.

I've tried everything, he said. Changing the code. Everything. You have a try if you want.

She stood there for a moment. Her blood was jumping and her head felt light, as if she was going to faint.

Go on, he said. Have a try.

She felt a prickle of sweat under her arms and, turning, she caught herself in the mirror. Her face looked like someone else's face – pale, dark-eyed, accusing. She glanced down at her hands. For a quick moment, she was certain she saw blood.

She swallowed and looked at him.

I don't want to, she said.

She put herself on the bed and shut her eyes. When she woke it was dark. She sat up quickly, taking breaths.

Whoa, he said. Why so jumpy? Take it easy.

She said nothing, listened for a moment. Outside, she could hear a steel band playing.

I think there's a party, he said.

She blinked at him.

It's in that bar place by the swimming pool. Cedric told me. He said we have to go.

He yawned. She saw that he'd poured himself a beer.

Let's not, he said. Let's just stay here.

No, she said. No. Let's go.

He looked surprised.

You really want to? Instead of staying here and getting room service? We could order something crappy. Snuggle up and watch TV.

She hesitated, her heart racing. She did not want to risk being trapped in the room with him.

We could go for a bit, she said. See what it's like?

He smiled at her, stood up and stretched.

OK, he said. It's a deal. And if we just can't bear it, we come back here and get room service.

She watched as he peered at himself in the mirror. Then he picked something up off the chest of drawers and laid it carefully on the low coffee table.

She tensed.

What's that?

Oh this? – he picked it up again and held it out to her – It was on the floor in the wardrobe. It must have come off a chain. Could be silver. Someone must have lost it. I don't know if it's valuable but I thought I ought to hand it in at reception.

Rachel stared at the tiny cross. She felt her bones go soft.

It probably belonged to the people who were in this room before us, he said. Or else one of the maids dropped it.

How do you know that?

He turned and looked at her for a moment, then he smiled.

Well, I know it's not yours. Unless you've gone and taken holy vows without telling me, that is?

Trying to smile, she shook her head. Watching as he replaced it on the coffee table.

Dan squirted on some cologne.

What did she say anyway? she asked him, forcing her eyes away from the cross.

What did who say?

He paused mid-squirt, his face suddenly smooth and relaxed and attentive.

Tash. What did she say?

He put down the cologne.

Oh, he said. Not a lot. But – poor girl – the press have now got hold of the thing about the other person in the car. Inevitably, I suppose. It's so upsetting for her –

He straightened up, tucking his shirt in.

I didn't know what to say. I suppose all I can do is

try and be a friend, you know, let her talk —

Blow off steam? Rachel said.

He looked at her for a second and then he smiled.

That's right. She blew off quite a bit with me today, actually.

That's good, Rachel said. That you can be such a friend.

He ran his hands through his hair.

I do my best. Now, how long do you think it'll take you to get ready? Should I have a quick cigarette?

Rachel thought about Dan and Natasha, talking and talking, blowing off steam. Her body felt as if it was made of air.

I'm ready now, she said and she slid off the bed and stood up and glanced at herself in the mirror.

The front of her dress was dark and dripping, slicked with blood.

She didn't know what happened next. She must have screamed or done something else dramatic and loud, because soon people were knocking on their door. Knock, knock, knock. High women's voices. The up-and-down tone of someone enquiring —

She heard Dan's voice, calm and convincing, thanking

them, saying that everything was all right. The door closing again.

He came back to her. She was lying flat on her back on the bed. Hands stiff and still by her side like a corpse. He touched her hair, her face, her clothes. All of them bone dry and bloodless and clean. She didn't move. She didn't dare.

I'm going mad, aren't I? she said. There's something wrong with me. There has to be. What if it's blood pressure or something? Pre-eclampsia? Seriously, do you think I should see a doctor?

He got the thin, shiny bed cover and pulled it up over her.

You haven't got pre-eclampsia. But I think I might ban you from reading that bloody pregnancy bible. And going off on walks all on your own.

She pushed the horrible cover off, blinked back tears.

But do you think it's having an effect on the baby? What if the baby's not OK?

He smiled, pulled the chair up to the bed. She watched his face. Playing for time. At last he sighed and shook his head.

You're overwrought, that's all. I'm sure it's not that unusual. But you do need to calm down a bit.

Calm down. Her heart fluttered. She ignored it —

lifted her head to get a look at her dress. Afraid even now of what she might see.

It was there, she told him. I saw it.

He kept his eyes on her.

It wasn't there. It isn't there. Your brain told you that there was blood. But there is no blood. End of story. The mind is a strange beast, Rach. You know that.

She swallowed.

So it's me. I'm going crazy. Seeing things.

He took a breath as if he was about to speak.

What? she said. Go on. Spit it out.

He shook his head.

I'm not saying anything.

She shut her eyes. More for company than anything else, she put a hand on her belly. She felt it straight away – the small, snagging movement. Quick and alive.

I don't know what's wrong with me, she whispered. I'm afraid of everything. I'm even afraid of this room.

He tried to laugh.

This room? What's this room ever done to you?

She looked around her. Everything was more or less in shadow now. Just a pool of light around the lamp. The glow of Dan's laptop. Beyond it, the twinkle of lights in the bay.

She thought about Natasha, sitting in her cottage alone. She looked at him.

Do you love me, Dan?

He shook his head.

Now you really do sound mad, he said.

They went to the party. She insisted. She told him she had to get out and he didn't seem in the mood to question anything any more.

She got ready. Changed into a pink jersey dress she'd forgotten she'd packed. It clung satisfyingly to the faint curve where her baby was. He looked at her and nodded approval.

Earrings? he said.

Yes, she thought. Earrings.

She got out the little diamond drop ones that had belonged to his mother. He helped her put them on because her hands were still shaking. She knew he liked it when she wore those earrings. And, for a quick, transfixing second, she had a vision of his mother, clip-clopping across a room in high heels and a tight skirt, slightly drunk perhaps on gin or vermouth, getting ready to go out on the town in her diamonds.

Dan smiled at her and told her she looked very nice

indeed. She tried to smile. She thought he probably did mean it. Then he picked up the key and they walked out of the room.

She did not look in the mirror on her way out.

The party was lively. A steel band was playing and a space had been cleared between the tables. Some people were already dancing. Shelley was one of them.

They found Mick and stood with him for a moment, none of them really saying anything. Then, before they could escape, Karen Keable had spotted them and was coming over. Rachel saw that she was wearing one of the kaftans from the shop. Purple with white stitching. Strappy metallic sandals that made her feet look like claws.

Don't go anywhere near the pool, she told them. There are men doing tricks. One's eating fire and another's chopping a lady in half. Very entertaining I'm sure, but a bit tasteless under the circumstances, don't you think?

Why? Dan said. What's tasteless about it?

Karen Keable gave him a look.

I'm sorry, but women being cut in half? Thanks very much, but I don't think that now is quite the time.

Mick let out a long breath and shook his head.

He's not big in the tact department, is he, old Cedric?

Karen Keable glanced around, then she lowered her voice.

They're now saying that she was definitely strangled. Choked the life out of her, he did.

Jeez, Mick said.

Cedric doesn't want people knowing. He wants to try and keep it quiet. But if you ask me I think that's a terrible idea.

I expect he doesn't want to scare the guests, Dan said.

Karen Keable made a face and again she looked at Rachel.

The guests aren't stupid. They're going to find out anyway. And some of us have been coming here for years. It's far worse in my opinion to have it hushed up.

She hesitated, still gazing at Rachel.

Are you all right, my dear? You're looking very pale.

I'm OK, Rachel said.

She took a small step away from the group. Her hands were shaking and suddenly she didn't trust them, so she folded her arms.

All the same, Karen Keable said, I wonder if you should sit down.

I'm fine, Rachel said. Really.

She's a bit anaemic, Dan said. I keep on trying to stuff steaks into her.

Rachel pretended to smile.

The band stopped playing and there was clapping. Suddenly Shelley was there, pink and breathless from the dancing. She pulled a cigarette from her handbag and held it out to Mick for a light. He held up both his hands.

Think I left it in the room, he said. Sorry.

Here – Dan felt in his pocket and brought his own lighter out – Don't whatever you do let my darling wife see this, because I keep on telling her I'm giving up –

Laughing, Shelley bent towards Dan's flame.

Hey! she said as she blew out smoke. You dropped something! Look – she pointed to the ground – It came out of your pocket.

Ah, Dan said as he bent down to get it. Well spotted. Mustn't lose this. I need to go and hand it in.

He held the little cross up and it glinted in the dark night air. Rachel swallowed, tried to look away.

Lost property, he explained. Well, I'm guessing any - way. I found it in our room. You never know, it might be important to someone. Sentimental value anyway.

He waved the thing around. Rachel wished he wouldn't.

Just put it away, she said to Dan. Please.

But he didn't put it away. He carried on standing there, gazing stupidly down at it in the palm of his hand. Meanwhile Karen Keable was staring at Rachel.

Your face, my dear. Seriously. You really don't look well at all. Are you sure you shouldn't sit down? Don't you think, Shelley, she's white as a sheet —

Here you go, said Mick.

He dived across to a nearby table and pulled over a chair. Still holding his drink in one hand, he put the other on Rachel's shoulder, hoping to get her to sit. To force her down. How dare he?

Rachel tore her eyes from Dan and the cross and fixed them on Mick.

Shelley screamed as the glass in Mick's hand exploded, splintered shards flying in all directions, beer sloshing into his face. He staggered backwards. Liquid streaming down the back of his T-shirt.

Rachel pushed her hair — a shock of black hair now — out of her face. Her hands were raw, bloody, the nails rimmed with dirt. She watched, her heart banging, as everyone rushed to Mick.

It wasn't me, she whispered over and over. You have to believe me. It was an accident. He did it to himself.

I didn't touch him or his stupid glass.

Karen Keable was gazing at her in fear and shock.

What the fuck's going on? Shelley cried, as Rachel took a quick, angry step towards her. But Dan had already got her, was steering her away.

I'm so incredibly sorry, he said. She really isn't well. Come on, my darling, let's get you sitting down somewhere.

They sat on some plastic chairs by the swimming pool. The tang of chlorine mixed with burning fat from the barbecue. Children charging up and down and screaming as the fire-eater swallowed his flaming torch. The band had started up again. Somewhere far away a dog was barking.

He kept his hand on her.

Don't, she said. Don't touch me.

He sighed.

Don't push me away, Rach. All I'm trying to do is calm you down.

He tried to rub her back and she pushed him off again. She leaned forward in her chair, propped her head in her hands.

I didn't do that, she said. What happened just then, it wasn't me.

She heard his breath, knew he was staring at her.

What exactly do you think happened? he said.

She blinked. Thought for a moment. Trying to get her ideas straight.

It's not your fault, she said at last.

Oh good, he said. I'm glad we've established that.

She ignored him.

There's someone here, she said. He wants me.

She heard Dan laugh.

Well, can you please show me where he is, because I'll bloody well knock his block off. And I'm sure Mick will be very happy to help.

She lifted her head, looked at him.

It's him. The man you were at school with. Hamilton.

She saw his face tense.

But I told you, I don't remember anyone called Hamilton. He's probably making it all up.

Rachel looked at him.

Why would he make it up?

Dan sighed.

For god's sake. I don't know, Rach. He probably wanted to – he was probably flirting with you, OK?

Flirting?

Yes. Trying to get your attention. Chatting you up. Some people think pregnant women are hot, you know.

Rachel said nothing. She did not know what to say. She shut her eyes and saw a villa high on the rocks. A bright, cobalt-blue-painted veranda. Purple bougain - villea tumbling down. Her heart began to thud.

No, she said. You're wrong. He does know you. From school. And he's here. And he wants something.

She glanced around – at the pool, the running, shouting children, the smoke and the darkness. Suddenly afraid.

But Dan was shaking his head.

If the guy's really here, then how come I've never seen him?

You don't believe me?

You keep on running into him – apparently. But I never do. Explain that. Shelley and Mick, too. How come they've never met him?

She looked at him, trembling.

It's not like that. Not exactly. He's not a guest at this resort.

Dan started to laugh.

I'm beginning to wish I wasn't one either. For fuck's sake, Rachel. What the hell do you mean?

She shut her eyes. Opened them again. She looked at him.

He's here, she said. He's here right now. He's –

She broke off. The air was suddenly chill, the sky

around them black and thick. Dan bent his head and put a hand on her knee.

OK. Let me get this straight. He's not a guest, but he's somehow here anyway. I'd like to know what they charge for that kind of guest. Does he get special rates, or what?

Rachel looked at him.

It's not funny.

She began to cry.

You've got to believe me. I can feel him, Dan. Right now. He's very close to us right now. This very minute.

Tears were pouring down her cheeks.

We have to go, she said. Tonight. We have to leave this place and go home. We have to, Dan. I don't want anything to happen to our baby.

He looked at her for a second, then he began to laugh again. He put his arm around her and pulled her closer. He carried on laughing. She could feel the vibration of his laughter in her bones, in their bones.

Oh Rachel, for god's sake, just stop. I mean it. What am I doing, encouraging you like this? Seriously, my darling, I just can't listen to any more of this – lunacy.

He kissed her.

Nothing's going to happen to our baby.

He held her face in his hands and he looked at her.

And anyway, we can't just go.

She stared at his face.

Why not? Why can't we?

He hesitated.

Apart from anything else, because we're in the middle of our honeymoon, that's why.

She kept her eyes on him.

What's the 'anything else'?

What?

What do you want? Why are we here? Why did you bring me here?

He didn't answer. Then he looked away and shook his head.

I won't do this, he said. I'm not going to get sucked into your – your – hormonal craziness.

Craziness? She touched where the baby was, felt the faintest, fizzy answering movement. She adjusted her face to make it look as if she thought Dan was right.

OK, she said. All right. I'm sorry. It's mad.

He didn't look at her. She knew he was fed up with her. When he spoke, his voice was still cold.

You said it.

I'm mad.

I didn't say that.

But I am, aren't I?

They were both silent for a moment or two. When he turned to her, his voice was careful.

Rachel, he said. I love you. And I like it here. It feels like paradise to me. But that's because of you, you know? You do that to me. I'm happy with you. It's why I married you. I'd be happy with you anywhere. The Arctic. Timbuktu. The fucking moon. Anywhere. All I need is for you to be happy too.

She said nothing. He touched her cheek.

Come on. Enough of sitting here. This music's a bit relentless, isn't it?

Yes, she said, though she didn't move.

We'll revert to plan B. Dinner in bed. We'll order steak frites. Or a cheeseburger. What about a cheeseburger?

Rachel watched a small, red-haired child go slap-slapping down the steps and along the edge of the pool in his sandals. She was suddenly aware of its vast dark expanse.

Yes, she said. I want to go. Can we go?

He hesitated, his eyes on her.

You OK to stand up?

I think so.

He pulled her up. She was still wobbly. He put his arm around her and they walked past the screaming kids and down the three or four steps which took them right along the edge of the pool. The water shivered in the light cast by the fire-eater's torch.

The water.

As they passed it, Rachel allowed herself to glance down into its depths just once, but that was enough. Because there it was. A long, dark human shape, lying there almost on the bottom. Black hair, dark clothes, white fingers and face. Rocking and twisting and swaying, pressed down by the weight of all that water.

She stopped and froze, every bone in her body stilled.

And then as she watched, everything grew sharper, tighter as, very slowly at first but then quicker and quicker, the whole thing came shooting up towards the surface, streaming up through the water, coming towards her, pale hands outstretched, reaching out for her –

Her screams must have been sudden and loud. Because the last thing she remembered was the look of terror on the face of the small red-haired boy as his mother yanked him away from her and carried him, wailing, up the steps.

Chapter Four

Cedric had them moved up to one of the private villas. Courtesy of the resort. Champagne and flowers. He said it was the least they could do, under the circumstances.

It isn't that, though, is it? Rachel said.

Isn't what?

He just wants me out of the way. So I don't frighten the other guests.

Dan sighed. His face was tired, unreadable.

I don't know what it is or it isn't, Rach, he said. And I don't really care. All I know is we've been upgraded to a fucking fantastic villa we could never normally have afforded and I intend to take full advantage and enjoy the rest of my holiday.

So there! Rachel silently added, as he strode out of

158

the spacious sitting room with its stupidly vast linen-covered sofa and dining table long enough to seat at least twenty people (let alone just two who were not planning on entertaining anyone at all) and out onto the majestic terrace with its bright, cobalt-blue-painted veranda which snaked right around the building and had the most blissful views out on to the foamy Atlantic Ocean.

It's glorious, Dan had said when they were first taken up there by one of the concierges and shown around. I can't get over the size of it. How about that, Rach? It's just like something out of one of your bloody magazines.

It's beautiful, Rachel said. I love it.

But it wasn't true. She didn't love it. There was something about it that she definitely did not love. She knew she would get no sympathy by mentioning it to Dan but, once or twice, standing on that blue veranda and looking out over the bougainvillea-covered wall, she'd seen the beach below, strewn with seaweed and foamy with waves, and had felt unsettled and raw. As if something deep inside her had gone irrevocably and inexplicably wrong.

Still, she knew he was right. They'd got lucky. They should try and enjoy it. And anyway none of it mattered now. She'd lost the will to worry or fight. All she wanted was to relax, not think or speak. To lie in the sun and daydream about her baby.

Dan had wanted her to see a doctor, and Cedric had told him there was someone on call, a man from St John's who was happy to come to the resort. But she refused.

I'm not ill, she said. And the baby's fine. What would I need a doctor for?

In fact, the baby was more than fine – a little more lively every day now, a definite and noticeable presence, fluttering inside her. The quickening, the book called it, and she liked the word. It made her think that he or she – Daphne or John or whoever it was growing inside her – was going to be a lively one. Quick and sharp and full of life.

All right, Dan said. But if anything else happens – anything at all, even the smallest thing – we get the doctor. No arguments.

Rachel said nothing. A small part of her registered the threat of the doctor as exactly that – a threat. But another part knew that Dan only had her welfare at heart. Hers and their baby's. Of course he did. It was no more than any concerned father-to-be would do, to threaten his wife with a doctor.

*

For two or three days, everything was calm. More than that, things actually seemed to lift and lighten. They forgot to be careful with each other and they had fun. Living as if they really were on holiday.

Dan had a tennis lesson, while she lay on their terrace – which she had to admit was gloriously quiet and comfortable, with its wide, glittering views of ocean and sky – and read her book. In fact she finished that one (which had won some prize or other, though frankly she couldn't see why) and began another. For the first time in a long time, she felt like she'd got possession of her brain again. She was her old self. The cacophony inside her head had died down and she could think.

And the beach. They got used to the seaweed and occasional jellyfish and began to relish the fact that the Atlantic side was a lot less crowded than Sugar Bay. They soon had a favourite umbrella and found that they could rely on getting it if Dan popped down straight after breakfast and draped his towel over one of the loungers.

Dan swam. Rachel swam – not as much as Dan, but she did. Dan laughed at her when she swam her careful, rigid breaststroke with her chin in the air. But what she liked most was to stand in the shallows, water nudging at her belly, and watch the tiny fish darting between her feet and feel the heat of the sunshine on her shoulders. Dan, meanwhile, would strike out and disappear for forty minutes at a time, sometimes going right around the rocks to the smoother waters on the other side and returning dripping and out of breath and full of stories of how crowded it was round there.

Mostly, though, they just lazed on the beach, fingers interlaced and feet touching. Rachel watched Dan's face as he listened to his iPod and smiled at the way his eyes twitched when it was a song he liked. Sometimes, watching him like that, her limbs loosened and warmed by the sun, she'd be surprised by a quick, hot stab of desire for him. Often, feeling lazy and comfortable, she let it pass. But once or twice, she told him about it and they ended up back in the preposterously large four-poster bed, and afterwards had to shake the sand from the sheets.

Another time, lying there in the heat of the day, half reading her book and half not, she happened to shade her eyes and glance up the cliff to where their villa was.

For a moment everything shuddered to a halt. She gazed at the low white wall with the bougainvillea tumbling over it, the bright cobalt blue of the veranda, the rattan sofa where she'd been sitting drinking coffee just an hour ago —

Dan – lying on his front turning the pages of a three-day-old newspaper – asked her what the matter was.

She didn't know. She struggled to remember what the matter was. Something wrapping itself tight around her. Her neck straining. The staleness of hair in her face –

She tried to take some breaths.

It's OK, she said. Just a funny feeling.

He said nothing. After a moment or two had passed, he reached out and caressed her thigh.

You and your funny feelings.

Dan thought about trying out a kayak, but decided against. Instead – and only because Karen Keable had been going on about it ever since they arrived – he agreed to play a game of tennis with Malcolm, who had recovered from his stomach trouble and was looking for a partner.

He doesn't look like he'd be capable of getting the ball over the net, Dan said. But I thought I should give him a chance. And if he's up for tennis, I suppose it at least proves she didn't eat him.

Rachel laughed. He told her she should go up to the spa and have a massage.

A massage?

Isn't there a little spa, up beyond the kids' play area? Go and see if they can give you a massage.

Rachel looked at him.

I don't know, she said.

He was standing behind her in his tennis gear. He came up and put his hands on her shoulders.

Go on, why not? It'd do you good. Isn't anything that relaxes you supposed to be good for the baby?

Rachel thought about this. It was true that the book said that massage released endorphins into the nervous system of the baby as well as the mother.

It'll be expensive, she said. And you probably have to book.

He bent to kiss her head.

You're worth it. Why don't you walk up there anyway? And if they can't do you now, then see if you can book it for tomorrow?

She looked at him.

You seem very eager to get rid of me.

He laughed.

I am. You rumbled me. I want to get Karen Keable over here for a romantic tryst.

It was almost midday by the time she got herself up

there. The heat was scorching and lizards skittered in and out of the cracks in the walls.

Spa Tranquillity, the sign said. Bamboo blinds and springy wooden floors. A smell of wax and lavender oil. She pushed the door open and for a moment she just stood there, stunned by the icy blast of the air-conditioning.

A woman in white trousers handed her a cup of herbal tea. She didn't want it, but she took it anyway. She explained about being pregnant and the woman looked at her and said she could fit her in right away.

What? Rachel said. You mean now?

The woman smiled. Her dark hair was twisted up on top of her head and pearls shone in her ears.

You look like you could do with it.

She gave Rachel a clipboard with a form to fill in, and handed her a biro. Then she disappeared behind a screen. The biro didn't work. Rachel thought briefly about leaving, but she didn't. Instead, she got up and went over to the desk and swapped the biro for another one.

She filled out the form, writing Dan's name down as next of kin, and his mobile number even though that was useless here on the island. She wrote that she'd had her appendix out but it was a long time ago and she couldn't remember the date. Under 'Other

Medical Conditions or Injuries not Listed', she hesitated for a second and then wrote Anxiety.

She undressed down to her knickers and lay on a couch that was covered with a white towel and a long strip of paper. The fan in the ceiling lifted the paper ever so slightly. There was a hole for her face.

You still OK on your front, my darling? the woman said as she tore the paper so Rachel could put her face in.

I think so, Rachel told her. The baby's begun to move quite a lot. I feel it most when I'm on my front.

Well, but that's nice, yes? To know your baby is alive and kicking?

Alive and kicking. Rachel smiled and tried to say that yes it was, but it was hard with her face in the hole.

The woman worked in silence for a while, pressing, kneading, sometimes just touching. There was some sort of piped music, but she soon stopped listening to it. She thought she heard the sea too, but that might have been in her head. She wondered if that was what it was like for the baby. The swoosh of all that amniotic fluid rushing around, soothing, rocking.

She felt herself begin to relax.

When at last the woman spoke to her, she had to

think for a second to remember where she was and what she was doing.

Afraid?

You are very afraid of something.

Rachel opened her eyes and looked at the floor. She saw the woman's toes, clean and unpainted in her white sandals, moving around her. Rocking backwards and forwards, calm and unhurried. She watched her move.

But why? she said.

The woman's fingers paused for a second.

Why?

Why would I be afraid?

The woman said nothing. She worked on in silence for a minute or so.

You believe in spirits? she said at last.

Rachel took a breath. The baby had just moved.

What? she said. You mean ghosts?

She felt the woman hesitate.

Not ghosts. Spirits. The spirit. It's the energy inside us all. Good energy, bad energy. The energy that continues after we are dead.

Bad energy. Rachel felt her heart speed up.

I don't know, she told the woman. Maybe.

The woman paused again. Her thumbs between Rachel's shoulder blades.

You are here with someone?

Yes, she said. My husband.

And he is a good man?

Rachel tried to think about Dan. For a quick moment, she couldn't even bring his face into her head.

Yes, she said. Yes, he is.

Again the woman's fingers paused.

There is something wrong here, she said. On the island.

Rachel took a breath.

You mean — ? She couldn't bring herself to talk about the murder.

The woman hesitated, then she sighed.

You need to look after him, she said. Your husband.

Rachel swallowed.

Look after him?

You need to be his eyes. Tell him not to turn his back on anyone. To stay alert.

Staring at the floor, Rachel couldn't help it. She smiled. The idea of trying to tell Dan something like that.

All right, she said. Thank you. I'll try and remem - ber that.

When she was dressed, the woman gave her a cup of

ice cold water. It was the coldest and best drink of water she'd ever had.

The woman was writing something down on a piece of paper. She held it out and Rachel stared at it.

It's me, the woman said. Sally. And that's where I live. It's near to this place. And my phone number. In case you need some help.

Rachel looked at her. The round, kind face. A wisp of hair come loose. The milky pearls in her lobes.

Why would I need help? she said.

The woman got up and came and sat on the chair beside Rachel and took her hand in both of hers. Her hands were cool and dry.

You wrote on the form that you suffer from anxiety.

Rachel put down the cup of water.

That's right, she said.

For a long time?

What?

When did it start, this anxiety?

Rachel tried to think.

I was quite anxious as a child. My father was an invalid. He'd had polio, you see, when he was young. I suppose I worried that he was going to die.

It sounded so stupid now when she said it aloud.

She looked at the woman and tried to laugh, but it didn't work.

The woman's face was serious.

And did he die?

Rachel thought about her father. His wheelchair. The special fleece cover on the back, flattened from use. The way it smelled of him, his sickroom smell. The bottles of medicines and pills. The lotions her mother rubbed on him to stop him getting sore. The shoes that were always perfectly clean and new from never being walked in.

She swallowed.

Not then. He died quite recently in fact. It was all right. He was eighty-six.

The woman looked at her.

A good age.

Yes.

All that worrying.

Rachel couldn't help it. She smiled.

Yes, she said again.

The woman frowned.

And when did you meet your husband?

Rachel hesitated.

Well, around the same time actually.

And that's when you became anxious again?

Rachel stared at her. The first real panic attack had

come about a month after her father died. About a week after she had met Dan.

She shut her eyes for a second, steadying herself, and saw it. The hole in the ground. The dark night. Dirt on her face —

She stood up fast, knocking the chair back against the flimsy table with its magazines. The woman reached out a hand to help her. Her eyes were full of sympathy and understanding. Rachel gathered herself

Yes, she said. You're right. It was exactly then.

She didn't tell Dan about any of the things the woman had said. She screwed up the piece of paper with her name and number on and chucked it into the grey, spiky bushes on her way back down to the villa.

How was the massage? Dan said.

He was already showered and changed, standing on the terrace, gulping down a bottle of Evian.

Rachel stood very still.

It was great. How was the tennis?

He made a face.

She went in the bedroom and shut the door. She stood for a moment, trying to remember why she'd come in. Then she went over to the big wardrobe where their empty suitcases were and she pushed the pearl stud which had somehow found its way into her pocket into one of the zip-up mesh compartments — under the book which she'd finished and the heavy cardigan which she'd worn on the plane.

After that, she wiped her hand on the side of her dress and then, thinking better of it, went and washed it properly with soap and water.

They ate a late, lazy lunch up at Rosi's. Sunlight pouring through the slatted roof, palm trees stirring in the breeze. Rachel had Thai chicken with rice, a green salad and two pieces of bread.

Dan leaned forward and tucked her hair behind her ear.

It's good to see you eating again.

She blinked, waiting for him to take his hand away.

I'm hungry, she said.

So I see.

He put his finger in his wine glass and fished out a bit of something. Then he stopped. Stared at the glass.

Damn, he said.

What?

Just — I forgot. I shouldn't be drinking this. Not if I'm going for a swim later.

Rachel looked at him.

Well, don't. Go for a swim, I mean. You're talking as if you have to.

He frowned at the table.

No. No, I do have to.

Why?

He thought for a second, then he looked up, grinned at her.

It's kind of a promise I made to myself. You know, to swim every day.

Rachel gazed at him.

So break it.

I can't.

Why not?

He shrugged. Made a face. Rachel noticed that it was the same face he used when he talked about Natasha. Careful, reasonable, righteous.

It's just the principle of the thing, he said. I know, I know. It sounds silly, doesn't it?

Rachel tried to cut her chicken but the knife was blunt. She tore at it with her fingers instead.

Yes, she said. It does.

Dan shrugged and she saw that his face had hardened.

I happen to love the water. Is that really so odd?

She heaped her fork with rice.

I don't know, she said.

Suddenly his face changed.

Quick, he said. Behind you!

She flushed and turned, her whole body tense. Dan was looking at her and shaking his head, laughing.

Jesus, Rach. Why so jumpy? Look — look who it is.

She looked.

One of the tiny starved cats from the other day was creeping towards them across the decking, its eyes narrowed and untrusting, its tail held rigid and aloft.

What are you going to do? he said. While I'm swimming?

He was walking up and down the terrace in a restless way, occasionally stopping and looking out at the sea. She yawned and smiled at him.

I don't know, she said. Does it matter?

He paused and sat down on the low wall. Frowning, he plucked a purple bougainvillea flower and started to pull it apart. He turned to face the sea again.

You should have a sleep, he said.

She watched the back of his head.

I don't feel like a sleep. I'm not the slightest bit tired.

It was true. She felt alert. Energised. Maybe this was the turnaround that the book talked about, around the beginning of the second trimester. She smiled to herself and instantly recognised the baby's fizzy presence.

Come here, she said. The baby's going crazy. Come on. I want you to see if you can feel it this time.

She stretched out an arm. He looked at her and hesitated.

Can I do it later?

What?

It's just that I'm a bit restless. Champing at the bit. Think I need my swim.

He picked up his cigarettes and his towel. Slung it over his shoulder. He didn't look at her.

You have a nap, he said. I won't be long.

She didn't have a nap. When he'd been gone at least twenty minutes, she pulled on her dress and a pair of sneakers and picked up her sunglasses and locked the villa and crept out along the snaking white path.

First she went down to the beach and stood at the bottom of the wooden steps. She looked around her. People were enjoying the last rays of afternoon sun - shine. Some kids were digging a big hole in the sand. Long shadows just beginning to creep up the beach.

There was no sign of Dan or his towel – not on

their usual lounger, not anywhere. She didn't know why she wasn't surprised, but she wasn't.

She retraced her steps and went back up past reception and then down again to the Sugar Bay side. The forecourt was dusty and deserted. Just a single police car and a handler who sat in the shade smoking and holding the lead of a panting dog.

She continued down past the Watersports Center, praying all the time that she wouldn't bump into Mick or Shelley who she hadn't seen since they moved to the villa and who, frankly, she wasn't missing at all.

It was warmer here and more crowded. A smell of fried fish came up from the grill place. She went past the souvenir stalls with their rows of bangles and clothes and carved animals.

A woman with hardly any teeth held a necklace out to her as she passed, but she smiled and shook her head and carried on walking. Halfway along the beach, she stopped. On a lounger quite close to the water was what looked like Dan's towel. She lifted it to check. Underneath were his cigarettes. She stood for a moment, shading her eyes and looking out to sea.

Lucky you, said a voice. I hear they moved you up to one of the villas?

She turned and saw Mr Keable sitting on a chair under an umbrella. He had on a pale straw hat and

some heavy, old-fashioned black swimming trunks.
His chest was white and sunken. He looked even older
without his clothes on.

She tried to look pleased to see him.

I know, she said. We were very lucky.

He stared at her.

I'm not keen on that beach, though. They have the
seaweed problem down there, don't they?

Rachel glanced back at the sea. She wondered how
quickly she could get away without seeming rude.

It's not too bad, she said.

He blinked.

Sargassum weed.

What?

That's what it is. From the Sargasso Sea. It rots on
the beach and stinks like the devil. Literally like the
devil. Gives off a kind of sulphurous gas, you see. Bad
eggs. You must have noticed?

Rachel turned and looked at him again.

I think they remove it, she said. Every morning.
These men come.

It was true. A couple of days ago, unable to sleep,
she'd sat on the terrace at dawn and watched as a
dozen young men, or boys, worked with rakes and
black bags, clearing it up.

Mr Keable rolled his eyes.

Ah yes. The men. If seven maids with seven mops swept it for half a year —

What? said Rachel.

He smiled.

Lewis Carroll.

He paused for a moment.

Incredibly bad for business, though, the weed. It drives all the tourists away. No one wants to sit on a beach that stinks, you see. Poor Cedric. Not to mention all this awful business with the girl.

Rachel looked at the sea again. She knew she could not bear to speak to him about Hortensia.

Anyway, she said. It's good to see you.

He picked up his newspaper.

Remember me to that nice husband of yours. Tell him I still intend to hold him to that game of tennis he promised me.

Rachel, already starting to walk away, froze.

But — I mean — didn't you play this morning?

He looked at her.

Oh no, my dear. I can't play yet. Haven't got a clean bill of health from the doctor, you see. Bloody man. But give me a day or two.

He put his paper down again.

By the way, if you're looking for him, I saw him just now.

What? she said.

Your husband. He's talking to that friend of his, the lady on the boat.

She turned to him.

What boat?

He seemed to have to think about it.

You know, the big catamaran thingy by the jetty. Is it a catamaran? Can't tell my arse from my elbow when it comes to boats.

He took off his sunglasses, rubbed at his eyes. Then put them back on. Looked at her.

He sees a lot of her, doesn't he? The tall blonde woman. Interested in boats, is he?

Rachel didn't know what to say.

I suppose she owns it. The boat? Don't see the attraction myself. Catamarans, I mean. A bit like riding a tricycle.

Rachel swallowed. Her hands were shaking.

They never tip over. No challenge. Why bother?

I know, Rachel said. It's silly, isn't it?

By the time she reached the villa, Dan was already there, sitting outside on the steps with his towel around his neck. He looked fed up.

Where on earth have you been?

Just for a walk.

Another of your walks? Well, you might have put the key under the step. I've been sitting here for about twenty minutes.

I'm sorry, she said. I forgot.

She took the key out of her pocket and handed it to him and he unlocked the door and they went inside. He shucked off his shoes and walked barefoot into the little open-plan kitchen. She heard him filling the kettle.

Tea?

What?

His head came around the white stone arch.

I said do you want a cup of tea?

No thanks, she said.

She went out and sat on the sofa on the terrace, her hands in her lap. She sat perfectly still for a moment or two. The baby was silent and still too.

Dan came padding back out, happy and energetic. Holding a white china cup with a Lipton teabag label on a string hanging out of it. He held the string and dunked the bag up and down, smiling at her.

You OK, my sweet?

Rachel said nothing. He sat down on the chair opposite her and fished out the bag and laid it carefully on the tiles. Water leaked out of it into the cracks. She watched as an ant, taken by surprise, was borne away.

Not really, she said.

He looked at her, his face still untroubled.

What?

I'm not OK.

Straight away, he put down the cup and came over and sat next to her. He touched the tip of her nose with a finger.

Hey, beautiful. Why aren't you OK? Tell me everything. What's up now?

She took a breath.

I ran into Mr Keable. On the beach just now. He said you didn't play tennis with him.

Dan looked at her for a second. He struck his forehead with his hand.

Oh god. I was going to tell you. No, he couldn't make it. He's still not up to it apparently. I played with someone else. This German guy.

Rachel was silent.

But you didn't tell me.

He sighed.

I'm sorry. I didn't really think of it.

Why?

It slipped my mind, OK? We went off and had lunch. You were full of your massage. We had other things to talk about. It didn't seem very important.

He paused, looking at her.

Christ, Rachel, how many more reasons do I have to come up with?

She swallowed, kept her eyes on him.

Who's your friend? she said.

He stared at her.

What?

The woman. On the boat. The woman you keep going to talk to.

Dan's eyes widened.

Sorry – I'm not with you. What woman?

She kept herself steady, watching his face.

There's a woman on a catamaran. She's tall and blonde. She owns the boat. When you go for your swims, you go and talk to her –

Dan began to laugh.

I don't know what you're talking about, he said.

Rachel tried to breathe.

You do. You do know what I'm talking about.

He was staring at her.

Seriously, darling, I haven't got a clue. What woman? What catamaran? Though if she's tall and blonde, I'd rather like to meet her.

She said nothing. She gazed at the tiles. Watched the ant recover itself and make its way, stupidly, straight back to the pool of spilt tea. Where several more ants joined it.

Dan got up and went back to his chair. When he spoke, his voice was low and certain.

When I go for my swims, I do exactly that. I swim. I never talk to anyone if I can help it. That's the whole point of swimming alone. I suppose I find it meditative or something.

She looked up and saw that he was watching her face.

What crime exactly are you accusing me of now? You're saying that when I go swimming I sometimes stop off and hang out with some blonde on a boat, is that it?

She kept her eyes on him.

Well, do you?

He shook his head, picked up his tea.

Rachel. This is crazy. I already told you.

Told me what? That it's not true? That you've never done it? Then say it. Look me in the eye and tell me you've never once since we've been on this island gone off and spoken to some woman on a catamaran.

He sipped his tea and looked at her.

Go on, she said. Say it.

No, he said. I won't.

Why not?

He put the cup down and stood up.

I'll tell you why not. Because I'm sick of trying to go along with all these crazy, fucked-up fantasies of yours. The way you question me about everything — every little detail, as if none of it adds up. I didn't remember to tell you that Malcolm Keable wasn't up to tennis, well so fucking what? And now there's some blonde I'm apparently seeing. For god's sake, you even act suspicious when I talk to Natasha. You'll be accusing me of having an affair with her next.

She gazed at his face. His beautiful face.

Well, are you? she said.

He said nothing. He made a noise of disgust and walked away, into the bedroom. Tears sprang to her eyes, but she continued to stare after him. Even when she heard the door click shut, she still kept her eyes on the space where his body had been.

She sat for a moment. She almost cried, but some - thing stopped her. After a few moments of sitting, something else made her get up and go to look out over the wall. The sun was almost gone. Shadows spilled over the water. The sea was black. She let herself look down at the deserted beach.

She knew he was there. She could feel it. Standing

looking up towards the villa, hands in pockets, black hair lifted by the wind. The face was whiter and more desolate than she'd ever seen it, pale and skeletal with its deep hollows and shadows. For once she wasn't surprised or afraid. She let herself gaze at him and their eyes seemed to meet for a moment or two. She kept her eyes there. Even when she felt her heart start to race, she still did nothing. She just stood there and watched him, let him watch her.

She turned briefly, listening for Dan. She didn't know what he was doing. Maybe he was already emailing Natasha. Or talking to her. Being supportive in the way that only Dan could be supportive.

She thought about the time straight after her father's death. She had been so fragile, so low, and Dan — his insistent and exhilarating attentiveness — had seemed a refuge. All the same, her mother had warned her. Don't rush into anything, not while you're like this. Wait until you're feeling stronger.

But he'd been so persistent. He had chased her, courted her, refused to take no for an answer. I know where you live, she remembered him saying when she tried, unsuccessfully, to push him away. I'll find you.

So she hadn't waited. She'd rushed right into it. Let him move into her flat and take over her life, and the next thing she knew they were having a baby. A wave of disgust swept over her. Her mother had been right. She'd done everything too quickly and without thinking. She sat down on the wall and put her head in her hands.

She sat there like that for a long time. Next time she looked, the beach was empty, the air white and sad.

Half an hour later, Dan came and found her. He'd showered. Put on a clean linen shirt. The cologne she'd bought him. His hair was slicked back the way she liked it.

He stood in front of her.

Are you even still speaking to me? he said.

She didn't answer. He sighed. Sat down and tried to take hold of her hand, but she pulled it away. At last, he bit his lip.

All right, he said. All right. You're such a sharp one, aren't you? Fucking hell, Rach. I can't get anything past you.

She allowed herself to look at him. He hesitated. She heard him swallow.

Though it pains me to admit it, you were right.

What? she said.

I lied to you.

Her mouth fell open. He shrugged.

OK? he said. Happy now?

She stared at him. She couldn't speak. He kept his eyes on hers for a moment, then he sighed.

She's called Julia. Julia Evans. And I suppose she is quite tall and quite blonde, though I don't really think of her like that. And she has one of the big cata - marans moored by the jetty — you remember we noticed them on the first night — ?

He broke off. Shook his head.

And — well, do I have to tell you any more? Because the thing is, a certain person has a birthday coming up. And I can tell you it's bloody hard trying to fix up a surprise for someone when you're spending every waking minute in her presence —

He broke off, grinning.

She gazed at him. She'd almost forgotten about her birthday. She was going to be thirty-two in — what? — a couple of days. The twenty-seventh.

Why don't you think of her like that? she said.

It was a stupid question, but she could not stop herself.

He was still smiling at her.

What?

This — Julia person. Why don't you think of her like that?

He shrugged, seeming genuinely to consider it.

I don't know. Does it matter? Oh for god's sake, Rachel, why even ask me that? You think I'd really go chasing after some woman on this island?

Rachel did not answer. She did not know what she thought.

So, you see, he was saying, I'm not such an evil man after all. Just a bit of a lousy surprise-arranger. I seem to have fucked up on all sides, don't I? Made you angry as well as spoiled the surprise.

He made a face. She tried to think about what he'd said. When she spoke, her voice was a whisper.

I'm sorry, she said. It's just, it never even — I mean, it didn't occur to me.

He seemed to brighten.

I was beginning to think I'd got away with it. That you'd forgotten all about your birthday.

It was true, she thought. She had. And everything he was saying made perfect sense, except —

She frowned.

But why did you say all those horrible things?

Horrible things?

Yes, about me having crazy fantasies and being suspicious of everything. It was so aggressive. Why did you have to do that?

He hung his head.

All right. Point taken. Maybe I was taking the whole cover-up operation thing a bit too far.

She still said nothing. At last, he held up his hands.

All right, I'm sorry. Sorry for being mean. It was wrong of me, and tasteless. For heaven's sake, what more do I have to do? Get down on the ground and lick your feet?

He fixed them drinks. Rum and Coke for him, lime and soda for her. He looked at her hard as he handed her the drink.

Look, honey, can you try and forget what I told you now? I really do want your birthday to contain some small element of surprise.

He emptied a bag of crisps into a bowl he'd found in one of the kitchen cupboards and held it out to her. She shook her head. He dived in and took a handful. She watched his face.

All right, she said. But I don't want to do anything.

What?

He looked up, surprised, his mouth full of crisps.

I want us to stay here. On my birthday. Just lie in the sun, do our usual thing. I don't want to go on any special trips or anything.

Dan was licking salt off his fingers. He frowned for

a second, then he shook his head and smiled.

Don't you worry about your birthday. I'm in charge of your birthday, OK?

She took a breath.

No, she said. It's not OK.

What do you mean?

I'm not going anywhere, Dan. I don't want to go on that woman's boat or catamaran or whatever – if that's what the surprise is supposed to be.

He looked startled.

But darling, why on earth not?

She shrugged. Tried to seem casual.

I don't know. I just don't want to.

He looked at her. Then he put down the bowl of crisps and came over. She knew he was going to touch her and she couldn't help it, she flinched. He didn't seem to notice.

Hey, he said. Where's all this coming from all of a sudden? Come on, don't be like that. I mean it. You don't have to worry about a thing. Just leave it to me, sweetheart.

He squeezed her shoulders, bent to kiss her head. His breath on her neck. She felt her heart speed up.

No, she pulled away out of his grasp. I don't want to leave it to you. I'm saying I don't want to do it. How many times do I have to say it, Dan? Do I have to be forced into doing something I don't want to do?

He let go of her at last. Hunched his shoulders and sat down.

Christ, he said. I don't know why you're doing this. It's really unkind.

She looked at him.

Why aren't you listening to me?

I am listening to you.

Then why don't you care even the tiniest bit about what I might actually want?

He seemed to think about this for a moment, but his eyes stayed cold.

I'm going to stop trying to arrange surprises for you.

Good, she said. Because I don't want surprises.

Fine, he said. I think I've got the point.

He picked up their glasses and was about to walk into the kitchen, when they both turned at an unfamiliar sound. Someone knocking on their door.

He put the glasses down and went to answer it. Rachel strained to listen and her heart sank. Seconds later Karen Keable came in. Even though she looked wild and pale and upset, she still managed to glance around, taking in the room, the furnishings, everything.

I'm ever so sorry to butt in, she said. You're probably trying to have a nice, relaxing evening —

She broke off and began openly to cry. Rachel stood up.

What is it? Are you all right?

Karen Keable shook her head.

It's happened again, she gasped. He's done it again. Whoever it is who's doing these awful —

She pulled a tissue from her sleeve and looked at Dan.

The terrible thing is, this time I knew her. Well, I say 'know', I didn't really know her. But I saw her just yesterday, when she did my feet.

Dan stared at her. Then he put a hand on her arm and guided her to a chair.

Who? he said. Who are you talking about?

Karen Keable sat down. She took a breath and looked at Rachel.

This afternoon. Just a few hours ago. That lovely girl from up at the spa. Sally. I can't believe it. She did my pedicure only yesterday. Did such a lovely, careful job. Such a pleasant girl. Chatting away about all sorts of things, we were.

What happened? Rachel said. Do you know what happened to her?

Karen Keable bit her lip.

Oh the same. Exactly the same as that other poor girl. Strangled. Just like the waitress. Except that this time it didn't even happen outside. A client came in and found her lying by the desk. She'd only come for a bit of electrolysis. Can you imagine the shock of finding that?

She was being buried alive. Earth piled on top of her, shovelfuls and shovelfuls of it. Dirt in her mouth, in her face, in her eyes, the weight of it on top of her, holding her down underground, she could not breathe, she could not breathe —

She woke. Saw the room, the walls. Curtains shifting in the night breeze. The clock's luminous numbers said 3.40. Her heart. It was banging so hard she was afraid the baby would feel it.

She looked around her for a moment. Then she picked up her glass, drank thirstily. Put it back on the table. Missed. It fell on the tiles and smashed.

Christ! Dan was immediately up, alert, next to her, grabbing her. Rachel? What the fuck are you doing?

She sat there on the edge of the bed, trembling. Her feet in a pool of water. Water and glass all over her feet.

Dan, she said. Dan.

Tears were pouring down her face.

*

He put on the light. Soothed her. Cleared everything up.

He picked up all the pieces of glass, the big ones and the small ones, and put them in the bin. Then he fetched a towel and wiped the floor. After that, he went and got another bath towel and folded it and laid it down by the side of the bed.

So you don't cut your feet, he said. We'll tell the cleaners in the morning and they'll do it properly.

She watched him as he took the bin full of glass back over to where it sat by the TV. He picked up the towel and folded and bunched it carefully in the corner by the door. Then he fetched her another glass of water. Clearing space on her bedside table so it wouldn't fall off.

Do you think you can possibly manage without this for the rest of the night? he said as he removed her pregnancy bible to make room for the water. He made a special thing of cradling it carefully in his arms as if he planned to rock it to sleep.

She couldn't help it, she laughed.

That's better, he said.

She looked at him standing there. Naked and tanned all over apart from the whiteness of his bottom. Hair sticking up, the marks of the pillow on the side of his face.

Thank you, she whispered.

He got back into bed. Threw her a look.

Don't be silly. What are you thanking me for?

She reached over and took a sip of the water.

For this. For being nice.

He punched his pillows back into the shape he liked.

Silly girl. Why on earth wouldn't I be nice? Come on, shut your eyes.

He stroked the side of her head with hands that were already clumsy with sleep.

She lay there looking at him. She saw that his eyes were closing.

I had such a terrible dream, she said.

Best not to think about it, then.

She sighed and shut her eyes. Opened them again. The bedside light was still on and the room was rosy and safe. Like the rooms of her childhood when her mother always left the landing light on.

Someone was putting me underground. This great huge hole in the ground. Pushing me in and putting earth on top of me. It was horrible –

His eyes snapped open.

What?

She blinked, watching him, watching her.

It was so horrible, she said again. I was so scared.

He gazed at her, frowning.

Funny dream to have.

I know.

He was silent a moment.

Where did that come from, then?

I don't know, she said.

She waited for him to say something else but instead he reached out, turned off the light. But she could tell from the sound of his breathing that he was wide awake now.

She didn't know what time it was when she woke. Early. Not even dawn. Violet sky. Barely light.

She got up to go to the bathroom, then crept back to bed hoping not to wake Dan, but he reached out for her. He tugged at her cotton slip and she helped him lift it, helped him take it off her. He groaned and rolled onto her, his body rough and urgent, his knee between her legs.

She smelled his breath, his body. Warm. Unwashed. He was pushing and pulling at her, but she stopped him. She put her hand on him and held him and got herself on top. She knew what to do. Almost as soon as she had got him inside her, it happened. She felt his quick, hot surprise and thought she heard him laugh. Or sob.

Rachel, he said.

He was wet all over afterwards. Sweat, or maybe not sweat. He pulled her down on him. Held on to her. And she let him. And they breathed together for a while and then, bit by bit, the breathing turned back into sleep.

The smell was the first thing that hit her. A wet, raw, metallic odour. In her nose, her mouth, at the back of her throat.

She opened her eyes. The curtains were parted and sunlight was in the room, making its juddery patterns on the wall. She saw all the familiar things. The lamp, the mirror, the bowl of fruit. Dan's pile of paper-backs. His jacket. Her bag. The table with its single orchid in a vase.

But the smell. It was everywhere. It had got to her stomach now. A stench of something watery, almost sweet. She felt herself start to gag.

The back of her hand, it was cold, so cold. Her wrist. Her shoulder. Her cotton slip that she must have somehow put back on in the night. Her whole body – or maybe not cold, but damp. Yes, wet. It was the sheet. The sheet was wet. She froze. She dared not move. She was lying in a pool of something –

Dan, she whispered.

Blood –

He didn't answer.

Blood – it was blood –

Dan!

Somehow, she got herself up. She forced herself from the bed and out – crawling, close to the floor, on hands and knees – out into the corridor with its dawn light, getting herself to the front door.

It was unlocked. She clawed at the catch, panicked, trembling. It took a while but she did it. Snatching at breaths, crying. She got herself out and onto the path.

She lay there, breathing. She just let herself breathe.

Her eyes saw pale gravel. Smooth and fleshy spikes of aloe vera. A small red beetle going about its business, wobbling along, oblivious. And a couple of waxy blossoms, fallen on the dry earth and already yellowing at their edges.

And the brightness. Bright hot sunlight. Morning.

She lay there, her cheek on the hard gravel, the sun beating down on her. She was dazzled. Burning. Safe. It was such a relief.

Chapter Five

The doctor was quite a young man. Almost a boy, in fact. But he moved in a convincing way. Touching her body with a light, careful authority. Writing notes with a ballpoint pen that made a pleasingly clicky sound. Asking her questions. Even the questions she couldn't answer, because he was a doctor, they still made sense. Just his presence in the room made her feel euphorically comfortable.

No one was sure how long she'd lain there.

I thought you'd gone off on another of your bloody walks, Dan had said.

Explaining how he'd woken up and found her gone, but thought nothing of it. Had a nice long shower. Pottered about a bit. Made himself a cup of coffee. Sat around on the terrace. Read his book. Even closed his eyes and had a snooze. While she lay out there on the path, stretched out on her side, burning.

The doctor put something cool on the burnt side of her. Soothing. Cold. It felt very good. Wonderful in fact. She asked him what it was. He seemed surprised, to hear her talking.

Aloe vera, he said.

Aloe vera?

She spoke the words aloud, testing them.

You've probably seen it growing on the island. It's one of nature's healers. It'll take the edge off the burning.

She widened her eyes.

Am I burning?

Not any more. But you were. I'll give you some Tylenol as well, for the pain.

But do I need it? she said. I can't feel anything at all.

He didn't look at her. He was holding her wrist and looking at his watch. She studied the side of his face – serious and intent.

That's the shock. Shielding you, for now. But it will hurt, I'm afraid. Later.

She heard Dan's voice.

You've got first degree burns, Rach. Your leg, your arm, your neck, your face, even your ear. That's what sunburn is, my darling. Serious burns.

Dan. Her husband. She felt herself stiffen. She kept herself turned away from him, kept her eyes on the doctor. His cool fingers. Holding her.

But is it safe? she asked him.

She meant for the baby. He looked at her.

Tylenol is perfectly safe.

She shut her eyes. Put a hand on the place where her baby was. Fizzing and floating. Looping the loop.

OK, she said. OK. Thank you.

But when Dan's mobile rang and he left the room, she seized the opportunity. She pushed herself up in the bed and fixed her eyes on the doctor.

Please, she said. Don't leave me alone with him.

He was doing up the buckles on his bag. He stopped and looked at her.

I don't feel safe, she said.

He tried to smile.

You're going to be all right. You don't need to worry. The shock of this will pass. You just need time. And in a few days the burns will heal.

It's not that, she said. It's him. He's planning something. I know he is.

The doctor looked at her carefully.

He cares about you very much, your husband. He is a good man, I think. A very nice man.

She blinked at him.

I know how it sounds, she said. And I know everyone thinks he's so nice. But I get these feelings that something bad is going to happen. Any moment now. Sometimes I can't even breathe.

The doctor came over and touched her wrist.

But you can. Look at you. You're breathing perfectly well right now.

She shook her head.

Sometimes I can't breathe and I think it's a warning. Someone's trying to warn me.

The doctor's face stayed steady. He moved away again and began to do up the other buckle on his bag.

Maybe you need to try and relax, he said.

She shut her eyes.

But it's real. I don't know if it's something that already happened, or that will happen. I can't tell you how frightened I am.

The doctor's face was serious now.

It will pass, he said. That feeling. I could give you something for it, but it's better to let it take its course. It's very common in these situations. I promise you it will pass.

*

So, Dan was in charge of her. She was in his care and at his mercy. For the moment there was nothing she could do about it.

How long do we have to stay here? she asked him when the doctor had gone. Because I want to go home. I don't mind at all if you want to stay. I can leave you here. I'd be quite happy to get on a plane and go home by myself.

He stared at her.

You honestly think I'm letting you go anywhere right now? The state you're in?

I'm trapped, then?

He looked pained.

Some people would call it trapped. And others would call it being cared for.

I don't want to be cared for.

He said nothing. He just shrugged, and he looked so forlorn that for a second or two she even doubted herself.

Am I losing my mind? she asked him. Tell me honestly. Is that what you think?

He touched her arm.

You've been through such a lot, darling. None of it is your fault. As soon as we get back home, we'll go and see someone.

Someone? What do you mean? Who will we see?

A doctor. A proper one.

That doctor's proper. He's good. I like him.

I mean someone who deals with – this. What you're suffering from.

She stared at him.

What am I suffering from?

He said nothing. She plucked at his T-shirt.

Tell me, she said.

He took a breath, reached out and gave her shoulder a squeeze.

You're tired, darling. You've been through such a lot. You need to rest.

I'm not even slightly tired.

We're in this together, Rach, he said.

She heard him later, talking on his phone in the other room. To Natasha, of course. She knew he was cup - ping the phone close, talking in a low voice, thinking she couldn't hear him. Did he think she was stupid, blind, deaf? It was so obvious that he was talking about her.

I know. Can't make sense of anything. Not a word. Three days. Three or four. Four at most.

Three or four days. What was going to happen in three or four days? She tensed, straining to listen.

So, she said when he came back in the room. What have the two of you decided?

He was holding his lighter and cigarettes, a sure sign he was planning to go off and sit on the terrace alone. He looked hassled, confused. He rubbed at his face.

What?

Who were you talking to? Was it Natasha? I heard you. I know you're planning something.

He came and sat down on the bed and looked at her. His face was careful, patient.

I had an email from Tash yesterday actually. I've been meaning to call her, but I haven't got around to it yet.

She watched his face. So clean and plausible.

So who were you talking to just now?

I wasn't talking to anyone.

I don't believe you. I heard you just now, chatting away.

He said nothing. He just gazed at her. Looked down at her leg. Her red, blistered leg. She looked at it too. It was her body but sometimes now it didn't feel like hers.

Are you in pain, darling? he said. Shall I get you something?

She shrugged and turned over, away from him. She

allowed her hand to creep over to the place where her baby was.

She thought about Daphne – or John or whoever it was – floating inside her. The ghostly curve of a pale, bald head. The small curled feet. The clenched baby fists. The eerie tangle of matter which joined them. She thought about how glad she was, to have the baby's company. It was a lifesaver. She would not want to be alone with this.

She heard him go into the kitchen to get the Tylenol and a glass of water. It was only as she heard him running the tap that she glanced at the table on his side of the bed, and saw that his phone was right there, along with his iPod and his half-read book.

For a couple of days, she did nothing. She lay in bed and she let him bring her things. A cup of tea. A glass of cold water. A peach that looked perfect but was rotten on the inside. And a plate of sandwiches ordered from room service, the filling (they both agreed) unidentifiable, the edges of the bread curling in the heat. She ate two bites and thought she was going to vomit. Dan threw them away.

Once, he brought her a small brandy. A bright, oily gobbet of liquid, slipping around in the bowl of the glass.

Drink it, he said. Go on. It might actually do you some good.

She sniffed at it, then – stupidly, why oh why? – did as he said and took a sip. Coughing as it went down her throat, burning. Its rough, sharp tang too much to bear. She gave it back to him, her hand on her throat, still coughing.

OK, he said as he took it back and placed it carefully on the chest of drawers. Never mind. Just thought it was worth a try.

She looked at him, her hand still on her throat.

Why do you want to kill me? she said.

She kept her eyes on him, waiting for an answer. His face didn't change.

Oh yes, he said. That's right. I want to kill you. I want to do away with you, don't I? I only brought you here to murder you. I want you gone.

She stared at him. He held her gaze for a second, then he started to laugh. Reached out and ruffled her hair.

For fuck's sake, Rach. Don't be such a bloody idiot. Let's just get you better so we can enjoy the rest of the holiday, OK?

She swallowed.

OK, she said.

The burns hurt, just as the doctor had said they would. A vigorous, smarting soreness which made her wince. She took the Tylenol but it didn't do much. Dan brought her cold, damp flannels, ice cubes wrapped in a cloth. The aloe vera was the only thing that made any difference.

And after the pain came the itching. It was a sensation she remembered from a long-ago childhood holiday when she'd been basted in Nivea cream by a well-meaning au pair and allowed to stay on the beach too long. The au pair had been sent packing and she'd cried all night — for the loss of the person who'd taught her Rummy and Hearts, as well as for the agony of the itching. It was an itching that made you feel sick. That made you shiver and shudder. That made you want to weep.

One time she did weep. Dan held her.

I bet you don't even know what day it is, he said.

What? she said.

He got up, held out a hand.

Stay right there.

He left the room and came back with a small yellow

cake on a plate. Its single wobbling flame was barely visible in the brilliant sunlight.

Happy birthday! You've missed half of it. But you were sleeping so peacefully, it seemed a shame to wake you.

She blew out the candle and he handed her a little box. She felt suddenly exhausted. She didn't want anything from him.

I'll open it later, she said.

No, he said. Don't be silly. Open it now.

In the end he did it for her. Pulled the thin gold chain from the hard black velvet pad. Undid the tiny gold clasp, fitted it around her neck.

He stepped back to look.

Perfect, he said. I knew it would be.

He fetched her a mirror. But when she looked, all she saw was the ghastly red mess of her face, the raw peeling skin on her cheekbone. The line of metal around her throat. Her feverish and frightened eyes.

There was no more talk, thank god, about a catamaran trip. He didn't mention it and neither did she. But whenever he left the villa — to go for a walk or a swim or, she couldn't help suspecting, to have one of his lengthy heart-to-hearts with Natasha or, presumably, the catamaran woman – she got out of bed and stalked the place, checking things.

Nothing she found reassured her.

The pearl stud she'd stowed away in the bottom of the suitcase was gone. It didn't surprise her. He must have rifled around among her things till he found it.

Her passport was gone too, and her plane ticket. In the end, feeling desperate, she asked him. He threw her a worried look.

But they're in the safe, he said. Where else would they be?

Can you get them out? Give me mine. I want to keep mine somewhere else.

His eyes were ungiving.

Don't be silly, darling. They need to stay in the safe. We'd be in a real pickle if we lost that stuff, you know that.

She looked at him. Very clever, she thought. Not for the first time, he looked upset.

What's this really about? he said.

She hugged herself.

I want to be in charge of my own stuff.

He sighed.

Look, we leave in ten days anyway. Surely it's OK if you let me take care of them till then?

Ten days. It seemed a lifetime. She had no idea how she would get herself and the baby through.

OK, she said. You're right. We'll leave them there. But just at least tell me the combination?

He looked at her for a second then he laughed.

Very funny, he said. Hilarious. You almost got me that time.

He went out onto the terrace and lay in the sun. She watched him for a while. And after that she watched a wasp that had flown into the room and got trapped against the window. It didn't sound like an insect at all, but a piece of electrical equipment about to explode. In the end she killed it. It was better that way.

One time she came across a cutting from one of the local papers. It had been folded up tight and placed in the pocket of a pair of shorts Dan hadn't worn in a few days.

Police Still Baffled By Resort Deaths was the headline. She read that police were still clueless as to the motive of a killer who had struck twice at the Wyndham's Resort in the space of a week. The two victims – Hortensia Batista, 17, a waitress who worked at the hotel, and Sally Lynch, 42, a beautician at the hotel's spa – had not known each other and detectives had been unable to uncover anything which might link them.

We haven't a clue what we're dealing with here, Police Commissioner Gary Lomax was quoted as saying. But we have faith in our excellent forensics team to help resolve matters as soon as possible.

Rachel read every word of the cutting, taking a careful look at the grainy photographs of both women. Then she folded it and stuffed it back in the pocket of the shorts. Ten minutes later, though, worried she might have folded it too carelessly and he'd know she'd read it, she went back and took it out and made sure to do it again, carefully and neatly, leaving it exactly how she'd found it.

Then she shook her head and laughed at herself. What did it matter if he knew she'd read it? Why was he hiding it from her anyway?

She noticed that he began to leave the villa more frequently.

You don't mind, do you? he said. Just I'm getting a bit cabin-feverish, cooped up in here.

She shook her head. She wasn't an invalid. How could she possibly mind?

Where are you going? she said, testing him.

He put his casual face on.

I'm going to see Mick and Shelley actually.

Rachel was surprised. She'd given them no thought in a very long time.

Are they still here? she said.

He smiled at her.

Of course they are. Why wouldn't they be?

But why do you need to see them?

He shrugged. Narrowed his eyes and blew smoke out of the side of his mouth.

Why? I don't know. I suppose I find them supportive. I need someone to talk to as well, you know.

She thought about this.

Does he hate me?

Who?

Mick. Has he forgiven me yet?

Dan picked a saucer up off the ground, flicked ash onto it. He glanced at her.

He's fine. And no one thought it was your fault, Rach. You know that.

She said nothing and he looked at her for another moment, a searching look. As if he was looking for something he was certain she could not give.

They're being very kind, you know. They were asking after you. They wanted to know how you were.

I'm absolutely fine, she said.

He nodded, but his eyes told another story.

I know, he said. I told them that.

Sometimes, now, when Dan was gone, she'd pad out, barefoot, onto the terrace and put her hands on the blue-painted rail with its tumbling purple flowers and let herself look out – at the sea, the sky and then, if she dared, at the beach below.

Sometimes she would just feel it – him – the shock of his presence, the tight feeling she'd get in her stomach when she didn't even have to scan the sand to sense him there, edging his slow way along the beach. Other times, though, he – it – was far more alive to her. She would see things. The shock of black hair, the grey wool suit, the small frisson of dread that she always experienced when he lifted his eyes to hers. What was he trying to tell her? And why? Why? Why?

The worst time of all, though, was when – left alone for an hour and feeling close to despair – she wandered into the kitchen to get something from the fridge and there he was, hanging from some kind of a hook on the ceiling.

His face was blueish and his eyes were open. A rough rope – it looked like one of the ropes they used to pull the kayaks in – pulled taut around his throat. She knew then that he'd been dead for a long time, years probably.

She staggered backwards and her heart thumped hard enough to burst out of her chest, but she forced herself to stay steady. She found it hard to look at him, but she did. She had to. She tried to keep her eyes on his poor, sad face and waited for a moment, half expecting him to speak to her.

But nothing happened and he still swung there and in the end she turned and, very slowly, putting one foot in front of the other and not letting herself look back, she left the room.

Chapter Six

In three or four days, her face was better. Her leg wasn't great and neither was her arm, but she kept them covered up.

She lay on the beach with her wide-brimmed sunhat and one of Dan's big linen shirts on. She liked the safety of the tent-like garment. She liked to imagine the baby jumping and twisting around, shrimp-like, beneath it.

You look positively regal, Dan said. Like some 1960s film star on the Riviera or something. Ava Gardner. Yes. A younger, prettier Ava Gardner.

She smiled at him. Then she laughed. It was important to let him think that she was OK. That things were back to normal now. But next time he stood up to go in the water – and she could see that he was itching to go – she told him she was going to have a little wander up to reception. To see if they had any nail polish remover in the shop.

It was obvious that he believed her.

Can you see if there's a newspaper while you're at it? Anything but the *Mail*. But only if it's less than three days old.

She took her time up there. She dawdled in the shop and looked at all the papers, but she didn't bother buying any because what was the point? They didn't have any nail polish remover, which was good. She didn't want it anyway and it would have been annoying to have to carry it around.

Next she went along to reception and, casually, as if she was thinking about booking one, asked for a list of the people who owned catamarans and offered trips. The girl – it wasn't the one called Marlene this time but someone a lot younger and stupider – gave her a couple of bright, printed leaflets. Quickly, Rachel turned them over, studying the names.

I was actually looking for one run by a woman, she said.

The girl didn't look very interested.

They've all got websites, she said. So if you want more info you can look them up next door.

Next door. Rachel knew where the Wi-Fi room was — she'd noticed people going in and out. Now it was almost empty, dim-lit and hushed and cool. Only one small kid in there playing a computer game.

She sat herself down at a screen and went through each website but, just as she expected, nothing came up. She was just about to give up and leave when — how could she have been so dense? — she remembered to do the obvious thing. She googled the name itself, along with 'Antigua' and 'catamaran'. She flushed and felt her heart begin to thump as she gazed at the screen.

That night they ate dinner at Riccardo's with Mick and Shelley. Dan told her he'd run into Mick on the beach and promised him he'd try and talk her into it.

They're concerned about you, he said. And they're off back home tomorrow. And we all thought it might do you some good, to get dressed up and eat a proper dinner for once.

Rachel waited until he'd finished listing reasons.

I don't mind seeing them, she said. In fact I'd like to.

He glanced up from fiddling with his shoelaces.

You've changed your tune.

She said nothing.

When they got to the restaurant, Mick and

Shelley were already there. She was several shades more tanned than when she'd last seen her and she smelled of a perfume so strong that Rachel could taste it in her mouth. Shelley jumped up and hugged her hard.

I'm not going to kiss you, she said. Because I've got lipstick on.

She took a step back and looked into Rachel's eyes. Squeezed her hand.

Look at you, she said. You look amazing. We've been thinking of you so much, you know. Trying to send good vibes.

Mick raised his glass.

Here's to you guys. The honeymooners.

He drank and looked at Dan.

Lucky sods. You did the right thing, coming for a good long stretch. I'd sell my soul for another week in this place. Or maybe not my soul but I'd certainly trade the wifey here.

Shelley laughed.

Forget it, babe. I somehow don't think I'm quite Cedric's kind of thing.

Mick scooped up a palmful of peanuts.

What's that supposed to mean?

He tossed them into his mouth. One of them missed and fell on the table. Shelley picked it up.

Oh come on. You really think Cedric's interested in the ladies?

Dan looked up from the wine list.

You're saying he's gay?

Shelley looked at Rachel and rolled her eyes.

Oh please. Come on, Rachel, isn't Cedric gay?

Rachel thought about Cedric. His eager eyes, his white suits, his constant, agitated movement.

I'm not sure what he is, she said. He's lonely, I think.

Shelley looked down at the table and straightened her knife and fork.

That's so true. Poor Cedric. He is. How clever of you to see it.

Rachel sees everything, Dan said.

They ordered a plate of grilled scallops to share for starters. Then Mick and the girls ordered swordfish kebabs and Dan said he'd have tuna on polenta.

Sounds good, Mick said and he twisted to look at the waiter. I think I might change my mind and have that instead.

Oh, damn you, Shelley said. Now you've got me thinking I made the wrong choice.

Dan put a hand on Rachel's knee.

Have the lobster, he whispered. You loved it before. You know it's what you want.

She shook her head. Even through the napkin,

the feel of him made her shake.

I don't want lobster, she said.

Shelley decided to stick with the swordfish. They all handed back their menus and sat and watched the fountain.

Mick told them all about the catamaran trip they'd gone on and thanked Dan for the tip. They hadn't hired it privately in the end, but they'd gone with just one other couple and it had been great, worth every penny. Even Shelley agreed that it had been fun.

We saw them catching marlin and tuna, she said. And wahoo.

Dan made a face.

Wahoo. I sometimes wish they'd catch a bit less wahoo.

Why? said Mick. What've you got against wahoo?

It's all you ever get to eat around here.

And we saw a shark, Shelley said.

Only a nursing shark, Mick said.

Nursing? You mean a nurse shark?

Whatever. One of them. Anyway – Mick turned to Dan – your mate, the lovely Julia, she's pretty impressive, isn't she? Skippering and all that.

Shelley tutted.

God, Mick. Listen to you –

Mick blinked.

What?

Well, that's so bloody sexist, isn't it?

What do you mean? What's sexist?

You mean for a woman. She's impressive for a woman.

Mick ignored Shelley and turned back to Dan.

How long's she been here anyway? She said she's from the UK originally.

Dan looked at him for a second.

Oh, I'm not sure. I mean, I don't know that much about her.

Mick looked surprised.

But I thought you guys knew each other from back home?

Hardly, Dan said. I've only met her a couple of times.

Mick frowned at his plate.

Seriously? Have I got it wrong, then? Only I could have sworn she said you knew people in common and all that.

Smiling, fingering the stem of his wine glass, Dan shook his head. Ran his hands through his hair.

I think she briefly went out with an old mate of mine. There's this chap who does a lot for the *FT*. Or used to. We met on a trip to Barbados. He's the one who told me about this place. That's probably what she meant.

Rachel sat back in her chair and looked at him. So at peace with himself and every single word he uttered that he was almost yawning. For a terrible moment she felt a strong urge to scream. But she tensed her jaw and managed to keep it in.

Halfway through the second course, Shelley leaned across and put a hand on her arm.

Hey, she said. Rachel? Are you OK?

Rachel glanced at Dan. He was looking around for the waiter, to ask for more wine. She looked at Shelley and was surprised to feel her eyes fill up. Shelley picked up her bag and felt around for a tissue.

Oh, you poor thing. What is it? What's the matter?

Rachel took the tissue Shelley gave her. She kept her eyes on Dan. He'd got the waiter now and was leaning back in his chair, pointing to something on the wine list.

She bit her lip and looked down at the tissue, folding it over and over. She swallowed back her tears.

Can I talk to you? Tomorrow. Before you go?

Shelley looked startled.

Why, what on earth's the matter?

Rachel shook her head and glanced at Dan again.

I can't say it. Not here. Can I come and see you?

Shelley was staring at her.

We leave at eleven. We've got a taxi coming.

Before that then?

OK. Sure. Any time from ten onwards. Half nine, even. We'll be up. You know where we are? Room Twenty-eight. The block just past the little pool, next to where you used to be.

She patted Rachel's wrist and Rachel glanced back at Dan. He was still talking to the waiter. As he turned and smiled at her, the candle at his elbow sputtered and went out. The waiter removed it quickly before the smoke went into his face.

She thought Dan had enjoyed himself and that he'd be relaxed given how much he'd had to drink. But back at the villa he seemed jumpy and on edge. He took a long time in the bathroom. Then he sat on the edge of the bed, frowning and flicking through the TV channels but not stopping on anything for more than three seconds.

She watched him.

What's wrong with you? she said.

He looked worn out. He tried to smile.

I don't know. I just don't think I'm sleepy yet.

Why not?

No reason really. It was a funny evening.

Funny in what way?

He shrugged.

I don't know. I think I'm going to sit outside and have one last little cigarette. You don't mind, do you?

She looked at him.

You want me to come?

She knew he'd say no.

Don't be silly. You're exhausted. You need to sleep. Go on, go to sleep. I won't be long.

He brushed his hand across her forehead and she tried not to shudder. She heard him go out. The sliding sound the door made as he opened it. The different sound of it half closing. And then, just discernible — or maybe she was imagining this — the click of his lighter.

She cleaned her teeth and got into bed and snapped the light off. She lay there, feeling the cool night air on her face and watching the half-drawn curtain as it lifted in the breeze. Filling and then relaxing, filling and then —

She didn't think she'd sleep. She didn't like the feeling of him out there and her in here, waiting for him to come in. She felt exposed, on edge. She thought she'd try and keep herself awake, lie there and think and listen and wonder about what she was going to say to Shelley in the morning, how she would explain it all, working it all out.

But she must have slept. Because minutes or maybe it was hours later, she woke to the sound of a chair being dragged across the terrace outside. She thought she heard a shout. Then felt a man's hard, heavy hands on her face.

The hands. They were pushing down on her and stopping her breath. She could not breathe. Her lungs, her chest — falling from a great height. Thick darkness. She thought that the curtains had been pulled closed. Trapping her. And her heart — her heart —

Not this. She did not want to die like this.

She screamed or tried to scream, but the hard heaviness of the hand came down over her mouth again. Briefly, she felt saliva on her — his or hers, she didn't know. Her blood was zigzagging around wildly now and she thought that some part of her was going to explode with the fear and panic of it.

At one point, sobbing hard and struggling to breathe, she must have opened her eyes because she thought, in the faint light that snuck in when the wind lifted the curtain, she saw what he was trying to do —

She screamed.

And then just as quickly and suddenly, it was over. He let go of her — she thought she remembered him pulling away with a sudden cry of surprise and pain. He was gone and, left alone in the room, in the black darkness, she knew only two things.

That for those few, terrible moments she'd forgot -
ten she was even having a baby. The baby might as well
have not existed. She had fought only for herself, this
one self, her own life.

The other thing she knew was that the bed was wet.

Jesus, Rach!

Dan was standing over her. His breath coming fast.
He'd put on the main light. Everything suddenly
raucously bright.

What's going on? What the hell are you doing?

She stared at him. His face was flushed. Red.
Drunk. He couldn't have been, but he looked it. She
stared at his eyes, his hands.

Are you all right? he said.

All right? Was she all right? She did not speak.
Instead she rolled over, trembling, and with some
difficulty got herself off the bed. He held out his
hands but she refused them and she noticed he did not
come to her.

She stood up. Wobbling a little. Trying to breathe.
Her feet on the tiles. The shame of the wetness
between her thighs.

Her cheek and her chin felt bruised. Her arm. Her

collarbone, was it? An ache like it had been stamped on. She tugged the damp sheets off the bed and, while he watched her, rolled them into a heap and threw them on the floor.

He looked bewildered. He was so convincing.

Darling, he said.

She looked at him. She did not know what would come next. What could he possibly do now? Her limbs were still trembling. They would not stay still. The shock. That was it. He made as if to touch her again, but again she pushed him away.

She wished she could stop shaking for just one single moment. She felt herself swallow. Her mouth dry.

What are you doing? she said at last. What is it you want to do?

When he still didn't speak, she took a step away from him and then she began to cry.

He looked at her for a long moment, a look as if he didn't know her at all. Then he sat down on the edge of the bed, put his head in his hands.

Oh, Rachel, he said. It's not me. I'm not trying to do anything. Can you really not see that it's all you?

She pulled on a clean T-shirt and fresh pyjama bottoms. A cardigan. She went through and sat on the sofa. Holding her spread-out fingers on the place where the baby was. Praying that she might feel even the smallest vibration of movement there.

He got her a glass of water. The glass slightly warm from the little dishwasher which the maid must have run when she came in to turn down their beds.

She held on to the warm glass and kept her other hand where the baby was and tried to keep herself afloat. Or not afloat exactly, but calm, strong. She had to be invincible now. For her baby's sake, this was it, the end. She had to cope.

Ah. There it was at last. The faint, but now familiar, movement. The baby, stretching, kicking. Thank god. She couldn't help it. She couldn't help it. She looked up and smiled.

Dan was watching her, his wrists on his knees.

The baby, she said. My baby's alive.

What?

It's kicking, she said.

The look on his face was pure terror.

Well, she thought, let him be afraid. He should be. He never wanted this child, but he won't kill it. Not on top of the people he's destroyed already. I won't let him.

He sighed. Fished in his pocket for cigarettes, pulled one out. He held it between his fingers. Looked at it as if he didn't care whether he smoked it or not. Then put it between his lips.

You'd better tell me, he said at last.

She watched his face.

Tell you what?

About the dream.

For a moment, she stared at him, uncomprehending. Then she got it. The dream. Of course. The dream. Looked at from his point of view, it all made perfect sense.

It was a botched attempt. Whatever he'd planned, for whatever reason, it had gone wrong. He must be furious. Distraught, even. But he could never, not in a million years, let her see that. His only hope, his only way out, was to pretend it had never happened.

She shivered. Pulled her cardigan close around her. OK. She could do that. If she had to. Yes. She could play that game.

She glanced at the door. Tried to remember whether it would be locked with the key or just on the inside latch. She tried to think about where her shoes were. Had she left them in the bedroom? Or under the chair in the hall? Shoes weren't vital though. She could go barefoot if she had to.

She looked down at her two bare feet. Tanned. White strips where her sandals had been. The dream. She took a breath, looked back at Dan.

It was so real, she said. I really thought it was happening. This man – in the dream I was sure it was you – he had his hands on me. He was trying to hurt me. Oh god, I was so afraid.

Dan was looking at her. Disbelief and concern on his face. He'd lit the cigarette and was taking a long drag on it.

Me? You dreamed I was hurting you?

She nodded, watching him.

Poor you, he said. Poor girl. There's so much going on in your head. You can't control these things.

Control. Yes, that was it. She looked at him. She held out her hands. She was still trembling.

But the bed, she said. When I woke up, the bed was wet.

Dan batted smoke away with his hand.

The bed? For god's sake, Rach. Don't worry about the bed.

I haven't wet the bed since I was a kid.

He shrugged.

It happens.

I'm sorry, she said.

Don't be ridiculous.

She watched him in silence.

I should have come to bed sooner, he said. I was

about to. I had a glass of that rum. Then I had another. I don't know why I had the second one. I didn't even want it. I was waiting for you to be properly asleep. I didn't want to wake you.

She listened to his lies. Then she leaned forward, touched his wrist.

Dan?

What, sweetheart?

I know this is me being completely over the top. But if we put the sheet to soak in the bath right now, then hang it out on the terrace overnight, it'll be dry by morning. The maid will never know.

He took another quick drag of his cigarette then stubbed it out. He glanced at her.

For goodness' sake. Don't start worrying about the staff. That's what they're here for, to clean up after you.

She tilted her head, pretending to consider this. Then she patted his wrist. Her blood was jumping now.

All the same. It would just make me feel a lot happier. Please, darling? Just go and run some water in the bath and put it in to soak for a bit? I can do the rest.

He sighed. Stood up.

I think you're being silly.

She smiled up at him.

I know. I'm a silly, paranoid and possibly delusional woman.

He looked at her. She liked that he couldn't tell whether she was joking or not. Deep inside her, the baby fizzed approval.

He went into the bedroom. She heard him open the door and walk through into the bathroom.

Just a few inches of water, she called after him. And try to swish it around a bit, give it a proper rinse.

She waited till she heard water crashing from the taps and then, not even stopping long enough to look around for her shoes, she jumped to her feet and she got the door open and she ran.

The night air hit her. Heavy with flowers pouring out their scent, loud with the rattle of cicadas, moon and stars barely showing through cloud. Dizzying. The openness of it all. She realised she had no idea what time it was. One? Two? Three? How long had she slept? The night had been going on for ever but the sky was still thick and black. She knew it was nowhere near dawn.

She hurried up the path, taking the left fork, making sure to keep herself in the shadows. It could only be a matter of minutes before he'd come after her. He'd come, yes he'd come, but he would not find her.

She was in some pain still, bruised and shaky, her shoulders and ribcage throbbing, but she wasn't going to think about that now. The baby was safe, which was all that mattered. Her heart was banging so hard she could feel it in her throat, but she ignored that too. Put all her energy into moving as fast as she could, away from the villa, away from him.

By the sign which said Tennis/Kidz Club, she stopped, confused. Her breath spilled out in gasps. She put her hands on the baby and struggled to think. What to do, what to do?

For a quick moment she considered going straight up to reception, asking whoever was on duty to call the police. But there might not be anyone there. And something told her that would be risky. Too much explaining. And those sullen girls. And the men in buff shirts with the dogs, they weren't reliable. And wouldn't they just call Dan anyway? And even if they didn't, wasn't reception one of the first places he'd think to come looking for her?

No, she needed to stick to her plan. She knew that the quickest way to Shelley and Mick's room was to follow the path that ran around the side of the swim - ming pool, but she didn't want to risk that in case it was lit. Anyway she hadn't been there at all since that terrible night. Horrible images skittered through her mind. She pushed them away.

No, she'd skirt around the other way, the long way, past the tennis courts and then —

Rachel!

It was him. He was coming after her. She started to run. At first the dirt path was soft under her feet, but then she hit the sudden sharpness of gravel — or was it glass? — but she could not let herself stop or cry out. She could not even allow herself to limp for fear of slowing down. Her eyes grew wet with the pain. Still she kept on.

Rachel, Rachel —

He wasn't shouting any more. Just calling. His voice barely even raised, calling to her, coaxing and wheedling, as if he was her friend. She tensed and strained to listen over the rattle of the insects and the thump of her heart. How far off was he?

A rustling in the bushes next to her made her jump, but she quickly realised it wasn't human. Mongoose, she thought. Or a lizard or a bird. Heart thudding, she moved back into the darkest part of the shadows and rested for a moment. She lifted her foot and touched it. It was sticky with blood.

She waited. The calling had stopped. Was this good or bad? She put her hand to her face and wiped tears away.

Oh, but she was so tired. All she really wanted to do was lie down and sleep. If it hadn't been for the baby –

She leaned back hard against the wall and shut her eyes for a second. When she opened them, she saw him. Just a foot or two away. He was wearing his grey wool suit and smiling his smile of the dead. Standing there. Waiting for her.

She almost cried out. But he shook his head, lifted a finger to his mouth. Very slowly, he took a step towards her, then another. Then he raised his hand and held it out to her. Long white fingers, long, dirty nails, his colourless palm turned upwards, inviting. She could not speak or think. She could do nothing. She reached out and gave him her hand.

The shock of his coldness was unlike anything she'd ever known. She had no defences against it. It went straight into her body, her belly, her blood.

Nothing happened for a moment or two. She held herself stiff and still, trying to breathe. He was closer now, still grasping her hand, pressing himself against her. His lips were on hers – was it a kiss? It wasn't like a kiss – then they moved down.

She held her breath, resisting for a second. Then something inside her just gave up. She felt herself relax. Let go. Relief as she let him in. Long before he said it, she knew what he'd say.

He took everything from me. You know that, Rachel. And now it's my turn. Now I'm taking everything from him.

It was Mick who came to the door. After what felt like ages of knocking, her thinking she would never manage to rouse them, that Dan would get there first and grab her and take her back to the villa before they let her in.

But Mick. Greying hair rough and loose, face astonished and unshaven. He looked older, angrier. She saw that the ponytail had covered a bald patch, and now there it was — the back of his head pale and shiny in contrast to the deep tan of his face. He stood there half asleep in boxers and T-shirt and gazed at her.

What the fuck?

She burst into tears.

In their room, fusty and sleep-smelling, sitting in the chair, holding a plastic cup of something they put into her hands — was it brandy? Just drink it, Shelley said — sitting there she caught a brief sight of her face in the mirror. Her own face. She couldn't believe what she saw. A person who was flushed and tangled and wild. A person who had nothing to do with her.

I know you must think I'm crazy, she told them,

unable to stop her teeth banging together with the adrenaline of it all. I know how it sounds. At first I didn't believe it either. None of it seemed to make any sense —

Shelley put a hand on her knee. She had on a pink satin robe with a stain on the hem. Panda eyes and alcohol breath.

Just try and calm down, she said.

Deep breaths, said Mick.

Rachel put her hands on her belly and she couldn't help it, she gasped.

You've got to help me. Please — I have no one else — I'm so scared —

She began to cry again.

Hush, Shelley said. It's all right.

Will you help me? she said.

Shelley looked at Mick.

Don't be daft. You're here now.

Mick yawned and picked up his watch off the table, looked at it, put it down again.

Just tell us what happened, Shelley said.

She tried to tell them everything in the exact right order, to get it out so it all fell straight and deft and true. But it was hard, in the middle of the night, to remember all the little details that made it properly convincing. Also, now that she heard herself saying it out loud, she worried about how some of it sounded.

I don't want you to think this is just about money, she said at one point when it felt like she'd already been talking for hours. But it can't be irrelevant that I met him straight after my father died? He would certainly have known about the money. There was no way he could have missed it. It was in all the papers.

Shelley gazed at her.

And you think he befriended you and asked you out because of that? And then married you and brought you here to kill you, so he could have your money?

Rachel's eyes welled up.

That's one hell of an accusation, said Mick.

Rachel put her hands to her face and began to sob.

I loved him, she said.

Shelley handed her a tissue.

Of course you did.

Rachel blinked and looked at her.

I didn't at first, you know. I wasn't sure about him. He had to convince me. But he did such a good job of it that — well — I fell so completely in love with him.

She saw Shelley look at Mick again.

But I should have trusted my instincts. I knew there was something. My mum didn't like him — and my mum likes everyone. Oh god, why didn't I just listen to my mum?

We all make mistakes, Shelley said.

The hardest part, of course, was telling them about Hamilton. She knew that the facts were there, if only she could make herself realise them. She shut her eyes for a moment, waiting and trusting that he would help her. When she finally looked at Shelley and spoke, she was amazed at how smoothly and easily it all came out. As if she'd always known it. As if nobody could possibly doubt that it made perfect sense.

Dan was a bully, she began, speaking as slowly and calmly as she could and trying her very hardest to sound balanced and fair. He tormented this poor boy at school. And I hate to say it, but I'm afraid Rufus was involved too –

Rufus? said Shelley. You mean Rufus Robinson?

Rachel nodded. She hesitated then, wondering whether now was the moment to bring up her suspicions about Natasha. She decided it could wait.

They did all sorts of cruel things to him, Dan and Rufus did, to this boy. And then one night they went too far. They dug a deep hole in the woods – as deep as a grave, it was – and they lured him there and they pushed him in and they started throwing dirt on him, trying to bury him alive –

Shelley shuddered.

That's my absolute worst fear. I can't think of anything worse, can you? Being buried alive.

Mick said nothing. Rachel looked at both their faces for a moment, catching her breath, anxious not to lose the thread.

The boy didn't die. He managed to get out. Luckily for them or it would have been murder. And he never told the teachers. I suppose he was afraid of what the two of them might do if he did. But it had a terrible effect on him. He was traumatised. He dropped out of school and he suffered from serious depression and a few years later he hanged himself. He was determined. He saw no way out but to die. He had a plan that if the hanging didn't work he would use his father's shotgun, but it never came to that. I'm only telling you that so you know how desperate he was.

How do you know that? Mick said.

What?

The stuff about what he was going to do if it didn't work? You make it sound as if you were there.

Rachel flushed to the roots of her hair.

I don't know how I know it. Who cares how I know it. I just do, OK?

Shelley flicked a glance at Mick, then back at her.

But Dan –

What about him?

Well – he must feel so terrible about that?

Rachel shrugged. Her cheeks were cooling. She felt calmer now.

I doubt he ever knew. Why would he? He and Rufus – they moved on and got on with their lives and forgot all about it. Dan doesn't know that I know any of this, by the way.

And how do you know it? Mick said again. That's what I mean. How come you know all of this, if it's something that happened to Dan a long time ago and he's never told you about it?

Rachel took a breath.

Well – this is the part you're going to find hard to believe. You remember the guy I told you about at the sunset drinks, at Shirley Heights? Hamilton. The man who'd lost his luggage?

Shelley frowned.

Hamilton? It doesn't ring any bells.

Mick looked blank.

Anyway, he said. What about him?

Rachel stared at him. She didn't like the briskness in his voice.

Honestly? Neither of you remember me telling you about him? How he had no holiday clothes with him and –

Shelley yawned.

Does it matter? Just tell us how he fits into this.

Rachel paused, more for effect than because she didn't know what to say next.

Well, Hamilton was the boy who Dan tried to bury alive.

Shelley's eyes widened.

What? And he's on holiday here? But — hold on — I thought you said he was dead?

Rachel drew a breath and rubbed her eyes.

I know. I know how it sounds. I can't really explain it either. But yes, it's him and yes, he's here —

Shelley looked at her.

Now? He's here now?

Rachel nodded.

I think he's been trying to warn me, you see. About Dan.

Mick had poured himself another large glass of brandy. He tried to pass the bottle to Shelley but she shook her head. He put a rough, hot hand on Rachel's arm. She tried not to mind it.

Hang on a minute. You're saying someone you met at Shirley Heights was in fact already dead? That you stood there chatting with a dead person?

Hardly surprising that they lost his luggage, then, Shelley added, looking at Mick, who began to laugh.

Rachel nodded, relieved. She tried to laugh too.

I know. It sounds ridiculous, doesn't it? And in a way he never really was here. I got reception to check. They have absolutely no record of him. And yet I saw him just now, tonight.

She put her face in her hands for a second. Felt her blood speed up. Looked up again at both of them.

I can't tell you how good it feels to be able to tell someone all of this at last.

They were all silent for a moment. Mick looked down at his drink.

But you still haven't told us how exactly he was planning to kill you.

Rachel shut her eyes, took a breath.

I can hardly bear to think about it. But he's been planning it ever since we got here — since before, I think. I thought it was odd that he'd already booked the holiday, without asking me. He said it was a surprise, but —

She sat up straight in the chair and looked at Mick.

Every time he said he was going for a swim, he wasn't swimming at all. He was seeing this woman — you know, the blonde woman, Julia, the one with the catamaran? Hanging out with her — chatting her up.

Making plans. And they were going to take me out in the catamaran, on my birthday – take me out into the middle of the sea, supposedly as a birthday treat, and then kill me. Drown me probably.

Shelley cupped a hand over her mouth. Rachel gave her a steady look.

It would have been so easy, to say it was an accident. I mean, who would have known any different? It completely scuppered it, of course, when I refused to go –

Excuse the pun, said Mick.

What?

Mick, Shelley said. Shut up.

Rachel looked at them both for a moment, confused. She took a breath.

But you know what I also discovered? That Julia woman, he's known her for years. She's an old girlfriend of his from back home.

What? said Shelley. You mean of Dan's?

Rachel nodded.

I knew the name was familiar. And I looked her up on the internet and that's when I realised. I recognised her. He has pictures of her in his old albums. She grew up in the same town. He's known her for years. So she must have been in on it from the start. She's probably the whole reason we came here to the island.

It was all part of the plan, I know that now. Maybe they were going to split the money. And I honestly wouldn't be surprised if Natasha was a part of it, too. Dan talks to her enough –

Shelley gasped.

Natasha! I don't believe it. There's no way she'd be a part of anything like this.

Rachel shrugged. She didn't want to think about Natasha right now.

And anyway, she continued. That's not the worst part. I haven't even told you the worst part. Do you know what happened tonight, after we left you? Dan waited till I'd gone to sleep and then he tried to do it – to kill me. I woke up to find his hands on my face and –

Shelley was staring at her.

Tonight? This happened tonight?

Rachel nodded.

Just now. Less than an hour ago. I think he was trying to strangle me.

Shelley looked at Mick again.

But – I don't understand – where is he now? What happened? Did he hurt you? What did he say?

Rachel tried to smile.

He said it was a dream. He said I'd dreamed it. The whole thing. Well, think about it. He had to, didn't he?

She saw Mick's face and she shivered.

I know, she said. I know what you're thinking. I can't prove it wasn't a dream. Don't worry, I'm not stupid. I know exactly how it sounds.

She swallowed. Looked around her. The room was dark, lit only by the light flung by the small bedside lamp. It was identical to the one she and Dan had been in, before the villa. For a moment she caught herself thinking of the cherry tomato. All the way from Gatwick. The way they'd laughed about it. A million years ago now, it seemed. Maybe it was still lying there where she'd thrown it, gleaming red among the bushes.

She shivered. She mustn't have any more brandy. It was going to her head. She put the glass down.

Mick was looking at Shelley. He let out a long, low whistle.

Well, he said. You wouldn't know it, would you, to look at the guy?

Shelley pulled a tissue from the box. Blew her nose.

He seems so nice, she said.

Just an all-round nice chap, Mick continued. That's what I thought the moment I met him. Like he's got his head screwed on, you know?

Rachel tensed.

You do believe me, don't you?

Shelley squeezed her arm.

Of course we do. But I'm sad to hear it. I thought you guys were so good together. You know, so much in love and on your honeymoon and everything.

He's never been in love with me, Rachel said. He wanted to marry me of course. That makes sense now. But he never wanted the baby. That messed things up. It was a genuine accident and of course he was dismayed when it happened.

There was a brief, tense silence.

All the same, he does seem to dote on you, Shelley said.

Mick nodded.

That first night, at the dinner here, you were all he talked about.

Rachel shook her head.

It's an act. A carefully crafted act. Don't you see? That's exactly what he wants you to think. The good man, the doting husband. I thought it too. Until I realised he'd been lying to me all this time.

Mick poured her more brandy. She tried to stop him, then she gave in. She wouldn't drink it. She watched it moving around, lighting up the glass.

He's lied to me, she said. And he's kept things from me. He's so convincing. He thinks of everything.

Well, he's a writer, isn't he? Mick said.

Rachel glanced at him. She hoped he wasn't too impressed by the writer thing.

Well, I don't believe a word he says any more, she said. Not in his writing and not in real life.

Fair enough, Shelley said.

Mick finished his drink and picked up his watch.

Look, ladies, I hate to break up the Halloween party but it's almost four in the morning.

Rachel stiffened.

You're not going to send me away?

Shelley stood up, pulled her robe around her. Rachel saw a large bruise on her leg.

Don't be silly, of course we aren't. Now that you've told us all this, we need to decide how best to help you.

Rachel looked at her, struggling to think straight.

I don't want the island police involved. Or Cedric. We need to get straight in touch with the British police. Maybe via an embassy? I know if I talk to them I can make them believe me. Do you think there's a way of doing that?

Shelley was shoving her feet into a pair of trainers.

There's bound to be. You leave it to us.

Rachel looked around her, suddenly afraid.

Please, I hate to be a nuisance, but can I stay here tonight? I just don't think I can feel safe anywhere else.

No one's going to make you go anywhere, Shelley said. Not unless it's somewhere you'll be safe.

She pulled a towel and a jacket and a couple of magazines off the sofa, and tossed one of the cushions onto the floor. She laid the remaining cushion flat like a pillow and patted it.

I want you to lie down here for a bit while Mick and I go and sort it all out. Will you do that for us, Rachel?

Rachel gazed at her and yawned.

I don't want to sleep.

It doesn't matter if you do. We'll wake you up.

Mick had put on a sweater and his hair was in a ponytail again. He reached down and patted her leg.

Just try and get some kip, he said. Seriously. Don't you worry about a thing.

Next time she opened her eyes, the room was no longer dark but flushed with colour. A slit of dawn sky showed through the gap in the curtains. On the floor she saw a striped canvas beach bag, a torn and creased copy of *Hello!* and a denim jacket. A pair of brown leather shoes. Unfamiliar things. Other people's things.

It took her a moment to remember. Mick and Shelley. The night. The brandy. How many hours had she slept? She realised she was cold. Her head hurt and her mouth was dry. She tried to stretch but her limbs would hardly move. She could hear a bird calling.

And now something else. The thing that had woken her. The sound of the door opening and then closing. Very softly. Just a click. And then – she heard Mick's voice, then Shelley's.

And Dan's.

She sat up. Heart racing. Heat shooting from the back of her neck to her fingertips. She thought she was going to be sick.

No, she said. Please. No.

Three of them. Three of them putting their hands on her, holding her, pushing her, telling her to be quiet.

She ignored them. She didn't do a single thing they asked. She carried on screaming. She did all that she could, the little that was in her power, to protect herself and her baby. Using her feet to kick them off, her nails, and, once or twice, her teeth. Several times, she heard Shelley cry out, shocked and upset. She heard Mick swear.

She did not hear Dan say anything.

At last, she curled herself into a tight ball in the furthest corner of the sofa and told them she'd only be quiet if they all took their hands off her.

Don't touch me, she said. I mean it. Get right away from me, all of you, and then I'll be quiet.

It worked. They all let go. Shelley's face was tense. Rachel saw her look at Dan.

What should we do? Should we get the doctor?

Mick was staring out of the window.

Stay out of it, Shelley. It's none of our business. It never was. Seriously, mate – he looked at Dan – maybe it's time you just took care of this?

Before Dan could speak, the phone rang. A single long ring. Shelley grabbed it. As she spoke, her eyes moved from Mick to Dan and back to Rachel again.

No, she said. Just a bad dream. I know. I will. Well, please apologise to – all right. Yes. Of course. Thank you.

She put the phone down. Looked at it for a second. Someone called the concierge.

Of course they did, Mick said. It's five in the fucking morning. She's probably woken the whole fucking resort.

Jesus, Mick, Shelley said. What's the matter with you? Can't you see she's in distress?

Mick threw himself down in a chair in the furthest corner of the room and yawned.

Rachel couldn't take her eyes off Shelley's face.

How could you? she said. The only reason I came here was because I thought I could trust you –

Shelley blew her nose and looked away.

I know you can't see it this way right now, Rachel. But we all care about you. I promise you, in the end it will be for the best.

It's for your own safety, Rachel, Mick said.

In the end. Her own safety. Rachel wanted to laugh, but she knew the laugh would do her no good. And meanwhile there was Dan. She realised he'd been edging closer. He was sitting on the floor, almost at the sofa. She raised her hands.

No, she told him. Get back. Get away from me.

He got up and went and sat on the edge of the low glass table. He looked forlorn, ashamed almost. An act. It was all an act. She felt like spitting at him.

Shelley was looking at him.

He's been so worried, she said. Haven't you, Dan? A couple of days ago he came to us and he was practically in tears, he was in such a state. All this stuff about you wanting to hurt yourself —

Rachel lifted her head and looked at Dan.

What? she said. What have you told them?

He shrugged.

What did you expect? he said. They were very concerned about you. And frankly, Rach, I needed someone to talk to. I don't think you realise how alone I've been.

Alone? she whispered.

With — all of this. I told you. They've been very kind. I didn't feel I could keep it from them.

Rachel stared at him.

What? Keep what from them?

She looked at Shelley.

What did he tell you? What did he say I did? Did he say I tried to kill myself?

Shelley bit her lip and looked away.

But it's not true! Rachel cried.

Dan sighed and got up and tried to come over to her, but she smacked him away. She looked at Shelley.

He's lying, she said. Whatever he's told you, it's not true. I've never tried to do anything like that. Not in a million years. I'm just not like that. I'm not that kind of person —

Shelley said nothing. She'd folded her arms and was looking sad.

You honestly think I'd kill myself, when there's a baby growing inside me?

There was a long silence then. A terrible, horrified silence that seemed to swallow up the whole room. Rachel looked at all their faces. Appalled. Pitying. She could not take her eyes off their faces.

I'm sorry, Rachel, Shelley said at last. Dan told us

about that too. I'm so very sorry. Really. Mick and I —
we both are.

Rachel felt the blood leave her face. When she
spoke, her voice was a whisper.

Told you about what?

No one spoke. No one said anything. The silence
was unbearable. Mick got up. Slid open the door to
the terrace. Stood with his back to them, looking out
at the dawn sky.

Shelley had tears in her eyes. She was looking at
Rachel. At last she took a breath.

My sister had two miscarriages, one after the other.
I was there the second time. It was worse than
anything I could have imagined. It was such a loss.
And at first she couldn't accept it either. It took her a
serious amount of time, to get over it. But she went on
to have three perfectly healthy kids.

Two boys and a girl. A real handful, they are.

She smiled at Rachel.

The eldest one's just done GCSEs.

Chapter Seven

By the time they got back to the villa, the sun was up. Early morning light on everything – the backs of the chairs on the terrace, the low stone wall, the purple blooms of the bougainvillea, the cold, wrinkled surface of the sea.

Rachel went into the bedroom and put herself on the bed. Her limbs felt cold and heavy, as if they didn't belong to her. Someone else's limbs. Pointless and apart. She shut her eyes.

Dan came in.

Just do it, she said to him. Get it over with. Whatever you want to do. I don't care. Just do it.

He stood looking down at her. She did not know what she saw in his face. She did not know whether it frightened her or not, and she did not care.

*

He went over and, in one quick movement, pulled open the curtains. She flinched as sunshine zigzagged across the room, greedy for access, exploding into every crack and corner. She heard beach noises. The far-off drone of a motorboat. Children laughing and shrieking.

They watched each other in silence.

Why did you lie to me? she said at last.

What?

About Julia.

She saw his face tense.

I didn't lie. I never told you a lie. I just didn't tell you it was her.

She paused, feeling her mind collect itself.

But it's why we came here, isn't it? So you could be with her.

Now Dan threw her a look of guilty amazement. It was quite satisfying.

For god's sake, Rachel. What on earth do you mean? It was a coincidence. I had no idea she was here till I ran into her on the beach.

She turned away from him, disgusted. She lay there and watched the sun making its bobbing patterns on the wall. He said nothing for a while. Then he sighed. When at last he spoke, his voice was tired, thick with emotion.

I don't know why I didn't tell you. Lots of reasons, I suppose. Partly I really did want it to be a surprise, about the catamaran, for your birthday. And also — well, all right, you want to know the truth? You've no idea how jumpy you've been, Rachel, how on edge. The way you question me, make me account for myself every second of the day. Every time I talk to Natasha —

Natasha. She felt her heart tighten.

You've lied to me, she said again. I don't care what you say. You're a liar. A liar and a bully. I can't trust you. I should never have trusted you.

She watched his face. Her thoughts were racing. She lay back down. Placed her two hands on the bed. The white coolness of the sheets.

Dan looked at her harder. His eyes were cold now. Stranger's eyes.

Tell me how you knew.

What?

About the boy from school, Hamilton. The stuff you told Shelley and Mick. Where did it all come from?

You don't deny it, then?

Dan turned to look out of the window.

I told you before. I barely remember him, but —

Barely? It's barely now, is it? When I asked you

about him before, in the restaurant, you told me you had absolutely no idea who he was. Another of your lies.

He looked at her and there was real pain on his face.

Not a lie, Rachel. I was telling the truth. It was a long time ago. I wasn't sure. About the name anyway. But — well, I think I do remember the incident.

The incident?

She almost laughed.

I honestly didn't know, Dan said, and she knew he was going out of his way to keep his voice measured and slow. About what happened to him later. And I don't know how you did. You say he's dead, and yet you spoke to him? Can you imagine how all of that sounds? Did you really expect Mick and Shelley to take you seriously?

Rachel said nothing. Instead, she lay back and watched the sun again.

You tormented him, she said at last. Both of you. You made his life miserable. You dug a hole and you put him in it. He was terrified. He could have died. You put him in that hole —

For a moment Dan almost looked afraid. He shut his eyes for a second.

I told you, before. A lot of bad things happened at school.

He swallowed.

I never meant to hurt him. None of us did. It was a stupid bit of fun. It was supposed to be a joke.

She felt her eyes widen.

A joke?

I was young and thoughtless, Rachel. So was Rufus. We both were. We hated ourselves and everyone else. I suppose these days it would probably have been taken more seriously. We'd have been chucked out, excluded, given counselling or whatever –

Counselling? You think you were the ones who needed help?

Dan shrugged and rubbed his face.

Fair enough. We probably just needed a bloody good hiding. But I think we were also desperate for attention, all of us were. We'd all in our own ways been neglected or deprived of parental attention one way or another.

Poor you, Rachel heard herself say. You poor things. I'm so very sorry.

Dan hesitated.

I didn't mean it like that. I'm not asking for your pity.

I'm not offering it.

He took a breath.

And that poor chap –

Hamilton, she said. It was Hamilton.

Dan gave her a quick, strange look.

He was just an easy target, I suppose. I hardly knew him. I hadn't thought about him in years until –

He broke off. Looked at her. She smiled.

Exactly, she said. Neither of you had. And you thought you'd got away with it. A clean getaway. Except that it's too late for Rufus now.

He gazed at her in real horror.

Rufus?

He should never have got into that car, should he?

You're not saying – Rachel – that Rufus, the accident –

Rachel smiled again. The truth was, she didn't know what she was saying. She no longer knew what she knew or didn't know. She felt suddenly wild, happy and hopeful. She was flying. She widened her eyes at Dan.

You were the one who told me there was a person in the car with him. You don't find that detail slightly worrying?

Dan was staring at her. She licked her lips. Watched as he took a step away from her.

How the hell do you know all of this?

She gazed out of the window. The sky was bright

with sunshine, soaring, cloudless. The most perfect blue she'd ever seen.

I don't know, she said. I don't know how I know it. I suppose it all just somehow came into my head.

After a minute or two, he got up and left the room. Good, she thought. But she heard him opening the fridge and pouring something. He came back in with two glasses, tried to hand her one.

When she wouldn't take it, he put it on the bedside table. She shuffled along in the bed, moving herself away from it.

Let me get this straight, he said. You're saying — you're implying — that a dear friend of mine is dead as a direct result of something that happened all those years ago?

She shook her head.

Not something that happened. Something you did.

He said nothing. He met her gaze for a moment and then he looked away. He put a hand out, touched her leg. She tried not to shrink from him. When he spoke, his voice was empty, tired.

You've been very ill, my darling. I'm not going to listen to any of this.

She shut her eyes.

Suit yourself, she said.

Seriously, he said. Your mind, it's been way out of kilter. Out of whack.

Whack. She thought about the word. She watched the fan go round and round.

Why did you tell Shelley and Mick that I tried to kill myself?

He met her gaze.

Because you did.

She swallowed. Shook her head.

You're lying —

He sighed.

You honestly don't remember? In the kitchen right here the other day? The rope?

She shivered. Thinking of Hamilton, swinging there. She put her hands to her throat.

Where on earth would I have got a rope?

God knows where you got it. We thought maybe you took it from one of the kayaks.

Rachel shook her head.

I didn't, she said. I didn't get a rope. You're lying. I never did that.

For a quick second, he met her eyes, then he looked away.

Rachel, he said. Haven't you seen yourself? Your neck. What do you think that mark is?

She stiffened. Put her hand to her throat again. She could not breathe.

No, she said. No.

She heard him sigh. She forced her mind to work.

If I was so ill, she said, then why didn't we leave? Why didn't you take me home?

He said nothing.

I begged you to let me go home. Why didn't you let me?

She heard him draw breath. Playing for time.

No one thought you were well enough to travel. I took advice from the doctor. He was very definite about it. So I thought we might as well stick it out.

They sat in silence, sunlight flickering over the wall. She waited, hoping that he'd go, but he didn't. Instead he just sat there, looking at her.

What? she said. What are you doing now?

He shrugged.

Nothing. Sitting here. Watching you.

What are you thinking?

His mouth twisted.

Nothing much. I don't know. Lots of things. Stuff about you, I suppose. About us.

What about us?

He shrugged.

Nothing that's coherent enough for me to tell you.

How convenient, she said.

He took a breath.

I suppose, more than anything, I'm thinking about how sad I feel.

She tried to smile.

Sad? What are you sad about?

He shook his head.

If I say it, you won't understand.

She continued to look at him and he sighed.

All right. When we met — you've no idea — I'd never met anyone like you, Rachel. You were, in the purest possible way, so unspoilt. Seriously, I was in awe. You'd only ever had good things in your life —

She shook her head. She knew exactly what he was doing. But he continued.

Good people, anyway. Even though you'd grown up with your father like that. Even though I know you were raw that night we met — still, you don't know how lucky you were — always surrounded by people who did their best, who loved you.

She thought about this.

Was I an easy target? she said.

What?

You said that Hamilton was an easy target. Was I an easy target?

He stared at the floor.

That's cruel, he said. I honestly don't know what you mean.

She said nothing. He lifted his head.

I loved you, Rachel. I loved you so much. I would have done anything for you. Anything.

And now?

He sighed a long sigh and ran his hands through his hair and shook his head.

What on earth do you think I'm doing right now?

She licked her lips and swallowed back tears. Trying to breathe. For a few minutes, neither of them spoke.

Is it really true? she asked him at last.

Is what true?

That our baby's dead?

He said nothing. She waited. She went on waiting. She thought he was never going to say anything. She thought she might scream with the waiting of it all.

Did I lose the baby? she said.

There was pain on his face. When he still didn't speak, she put her hands to her mouth, her eyes, her head. Noise began to come out of her. She let it come.

Through the gaps in her fingers, she could see the white expanse of the ceiling. The blunt wooden blades of the fan. The small silver chain that hung down.

Rachel, he said, but she turned herself over in the bed, away from him.

She felt him standing there looking at her for one more moment. Then she heard him turn and walk out of the room, shutting the door behind him.

For a long time, she did nothing. Just lay there, staring at the ceiling, feeling her whole body grow still. Letting him think she'd gone to sleep. Or left the villa. Or was taking a bath. Or anything really, whatever he liked. It didn't really matter what he thought.

She lay there for a very long time.

Then, when she thought enough time had passed — it might have been hours or it might have been days — she slid herself off the bed and crept to the bathroom and, picking up the heavy marble weight which kept the door wedged open and holding it in both of her hands, she walked out to the terrace with it.

He was sitting out there with his back to her. The way he'd sat a million times before. Or maybe not a million times. But a lot of times in the past however many days.

His slender bare feet up on the slatted wooden table, resting on one of the linen cushions he'd taken from the sofa. Next to them, his book, splayed open, face down. A bottle of sun oil with the cap off. An empty glass. A pack of cigarettes. A white coffee cup. The saucer that belonged to the cup, three cigarettes on it, half smoked and stubbed out.

He sat there motionless with his face turned to the sun. He did not hear her. He didn't turn around.

She stood for a moment, watching him. The familiar shape of his big toes, the slick of sun oil – ineptly applied because he hated the feel of it on his fingers – on his knees, shins and shoulders. The scattering of freckles on his upper arms. The little patches of soft, dark hair. The sudden, heartbreaking whiteness of the crease at the back of his neck.

For a quick, unnerving moment, she thought he looked exactly like her father – something about the boyish shoulders and curly back of the head – and she felt herself soften, dismayed. But she pushed the thought away, before it could take hold. He wasn't her father. He was nothing like her father. He never would be.

She edged forward. Moving her bare feet across the warm tiles, steady and noiseless and unseen. At one point she saw him raise his hand and brush something from his arm – and she stopped, breath held, weight on one leg. Then he dropped his arm again and she was able to move.

She thought she heard him sigh.

She moved closer.

His face was towards the sun and she imagined his eyes were closed. She saw that his head was tilted back, perfectly exposing his throat, and it briefly occurred to her that she ought to have got a knife. One of the small serrated ones they used for cutting lemons. But it was too late —

She was right behind him now, the marble weight in her hands, its sheer heft straining the tendons of her wrists. Before anything could happen to make her change her mind, she lifted it high above his head and with one quick movement, she struck.

The moment of impact. The whack, the crunch. She had no memory of it. Nor did she remember the next moment, nor the one after that. She did not recall him turning at the last minute in startled horror, as the weight missed the back of his skull and caught him instead on the chin. Grabbing at her with both of his hands, knocking the cup and the glass and then the cushion and then his book off the table. The terrible stricken look in his eyes. The caving of his mouth in fear and shock —

She missed all of that.

She did not see the blackish blood that drenched his hair as she got him properly the second time. Or feel the ripe fruit smash of his temple as she struck at it again. And again. And again. And she did not hear the howling, wailing sound that came tearing from his chest. A terrible, unlikely noise that didn't sound at all like the Dan she had loved —

She knew nothing of any of this.

Instead, suddenly, there he was — shockingly — right down there on the tiles. A terrible long snake of a man, dragging himself as fast as he could across that bright and sunny terrace, getting himself away from her on knees and belly and elbows. She saw that the bare soles of his feet were gritty and blackened, that his arms and legs flailed enough to leave a long, fanning smudge of blood in his wake.

She stared. And for a brief second or two, she thought she might leave him. Spare him. But a cold hand came down on her shoulder. Ice in her bones.

Follow him. Finish it.

All the same, when she saw the wound on his head — smashed open and bleeding, meat and gristle and bone — she couldn't help it, she gasped. Because she understood, then, what she'd done.

Dan! she cried.

She began to sob and sob, calling his name. She turned away, covered her eyes with her hands.

I can't do it! she cried. Don't make me do it!

Straight away he was there. It, him. Cold breath on her neck. The familiar sweet and pungent earth smell. His fingers propelling her —

You can, he whispered. You have to.

And she saw it, then. The black terror of that hole in the ground. The wet night air. Its deep, slippery sides. Earth falling on his face. In his mouth, up his nose, grit smashing against his teeth. His panicked cries as he realised he could not breathe and listened to the terrible rhythm of the spade, shovelling, throwing, shovelling, throwing —

He was inside her, now, a quickening, lively presence right in the very heart of her. He had her. She was his. She kept her eyes on the bloody, moving mess that was Dan and she did exactly as he told her, following him, the weight held high in her hands, stalking him as she would have stalked any not-quite-killed creature.

That's right, he said, guiding her.

Dan. The bully. He would not escape. She would finish him off. Just as she'd done the others. Speeding in the car with Rufus on that cold, starry night. The dawning horror of his cries as he tried to wrestle the wheel back from her, the satisfying crack as his breastbone slammed against the wheel, the final impact as the car hit the gate.

Hortensia, too. It hadn't been hard, to squeeze the life out of her. So sweet and guileless and unsus - pecting, with her little silver cross around her neck. What a laugh that was. She went cleanly and quickly, without a word, her heart just giving up in the vivid heat. Sally had been harder — a surprisingly vicious struggle on the scrubbed pine floor, nail polish bottles and manicure tools flying. She'd fought hard and dirty for such a gentle person and had no one but herself to blame for the fact that an earring had been ripped from her ear.

There was hardly any fight left in Dan now. She knew that as she slowed her pace to match his shambling crawl. She watched his poor, blood-drenched face. He had that puzzled look that he got when he couldn't figure something out. A recipe. An instruction manual. A crossword. She knew that face and it was breaking her heart — oh, she could not look at it any longer — so she decided to finish it.

Bending and striking him again, stepping back as he screamed and the blood spurted. She heard her own breath, panting, sobbing. He'd turned over onto his side now and was holding one hand up against his head and she thought he might be trying to speak to her, but nothing was coming out, only darkish bubbles, blood and air —

She could not bear it. She aimed for his mouth. Then his temple. Then his jaw. The hard curve of the back of his skull. She didn't need any help this time. She knew what to do. She swung the weight back and smashed it down, again and again and again and then once more, crying out as black liquid spurted through the blue air and his whole body shivered and went still.

She stepped back, away from what she had done. She swallowed, her breath coming in little jagged gasps.

He was gone. There was nothing. Dan was gone.

Silence. It was over. It was done. There was nothing more to do but to sit here, alone in the vicious morning heat, listening to the rattle of the cicadas in the purple bougainvillea, enjoying the crashing blueness of that Caribbean sky.

She sat down against the wall and, very gently, she laid the piece of marble on the ground. She took some breaths. Wiped her bloody hands as well as she could on her T-shirt and looked around her. It was hot. Very hot. The sun was high. Everything droning and buzzing. She watched an insect hang for a split second in the air above a dark oleander blossom, then fall inside, lost to view.

She looked at the sticky black mess of him, lying there. Then she thought better of it. She didn't look. She shut her eyes.

And then, placing her two hands on her belly, she waited to feel it. The thing she wanted to feel more than anything in the world. The fizz of tiny limbs. The sweet, quickening movement of her baby.

She waited.

And waited.

She didn't panic. She refused to. It might not mean anything. Babies slept, didn't they? How else would they ever muster the energy to develop and grow, hanging and floating there, cells multiplying, life ripening?

She thought of the little ship, safe in its bubble of liquid, gliding smoothly up and down, eerie, intact. And she lifted her bloodstained fingers and looked down at the small but definite curve of her belly.

I know you're in there somewhere, she said. Daphne or John or whoever you are.

Or Hamilton. What about that? It wasn't a bad name, now she thought about it. It had a certain ring.

She smiled to herself. Then she put her hands back on the place where she was certain her baby still was and, happy to wait for as long as it took, she turned her face to the sun.

Acknowledgements

Thank you to my phenomenally sharp editor, Selina Walker – aided by equally pinpoint work from Anna Jean Hughes and Deborah Adams – for helping me get down on paper exactly what was in my head. To Jonathan, Jake, Chloë and Raph for letting me go on (and on, and on) about ghosts for all these years. And to my mum whose knack for clocking the eerie, the ambiguous and the unexplained – and telling it in a way that at the time seemed ordinary, but which I now realise was a gift – is a huge part of how I turned into a writer.

JSM

IF YOU LIKED *THE QUICKENING*
THEN YOU MIGHT ENJOY *CAT OUT OF HELL*

By acclaimed storyteller Lynne Truss, author of the bestselling *Eats, Shoots & Leaves*, the mesmerising tale of a cat with nine lives, and a relationship as ancient as time itself and just as powerful.

The scene: a cottage on the coast on a windy evening. Inside, a room with curtains drawn. Tea has just been made. A kettle still steams.

Under a pool of yellow light, two figures face each other across a kitchen table. A man and a cat.

The story about to be related is so unusual yet so terrifyingly plausible that it demands to be told in a single sitting.

The man clears his throat, and leans forward, expectant.

'Shall we begin?' says the cat ...

About Hammer

Hammer is the most well-known film brand in the UK, having made over 150 feature films which have been terrifying and thrilling audiences worldwide for generations.

Whilst synonymous with horror and the genre-defining classics it produced in the 1950s to 1970s, Hammer was recently rebooted in the film world as the home of "Smart Horror", with the critically acclaimed *Let Me In* and *The Woman in Black*. With *The Woman in Black: Angel of Death* scheduled for 2014, Hammer has been re-born.

Hammer's literary legacy is also now being revived through its new partnership with Arrow Books. This series features original novellas by some of today's most celebrated authors, as well as classic stories from nearly a century of production.

In 2014 Hammer Arrow will publish books by DBC Pierre, Lynne Truss and Joanna Briscoe as well as a novelisation of the forthcoming *The Woman in Black: Angel of Death*, continuing a programme that began with bestselling novellas from Helen Dunmore and Jeanette Winterson. Beautifully produced and written to read in a single sitting, Hammer Arrow books are perfect for readers of quality contemporary fiction.

For more information on Hammer
visit: www.hammerfilms.com or
www.facebook.com/hammerfilms